Hellish Ascent
THE HELLBORN SERIES
BOOK TWO

NATHAN SQUIERS

Copyright © 2024 by Nathan Squiers

All rights reserved.

No part of this book may be reproduced in any form or by any electronic or mechanical means, including information storage and retrieval systems, without written permission from the author, except for the use of brief quotations in a book review.

Cover design by: EmCat Designs

Formatted by: EmCat Designs

"Th-that's... **MINE!***"*
 Varian

> *CEASE, QUEEN,*
> *LEST THE VERMIN AND DEGENERATES*
> *VENTURE TO EMBOLDEN THEMSELVES!*
> ???

CHAPTER 1
DETECTIVE DEXTER IS ON THE CASE

Felicia still wasn't home.

The first few slices from this truth-pie were bitter but to-the-point: the first slice being that Felicia didn't *need* to be home; didn't *need* to come home every night. Felicia, as both she and others had told Dexter before, was "a big girl" and, as such, "could take care of herself." Dexter understood this, and, in his own Dexter-ish way, he respected it. Dexter's respect for Felicia being "a big girl" and the fact that she could "take care of herself," however, were "droplets of water in an otherwise empty glass." That was how Felicia had described it, at least. Dexter wasn't sure he agreed; wasn't sure he respected *that* perspective.

And, since he respected a fair amount of Felicia's perspectives, Dexter couldn't help but think he was owed some arguing rights when he *didn't*. He agreed and respected that Felicia was "a big girl" who could "take care of herself," but why should any of that matter when a *bigger* man could step in and take care of her *better?* This, however, was a perspective that Felicia and others had *aggressively* disagreed with and disrespected right to Dexter's face.

That was why the next few slices from that truth-pie were especially bitter.

One slice in particular—*maybe the reason Felicia still wasn't home was because of Dexter; because she was asserting that she was "a big girl" who "could take care of herself"*—tasted especially personal. Dexter didn't like that slice of pie at all, but there were a few other slices, sweeter ones, that spoke against this theory. For one, it was Thursday, and Felicia had her math and English classes on Tuesdays and Thursdays. That part of the truth-pie wasn't coated in a whipped topping of theory—that was *fact*. Also a fact: Felicia's math and English books were still in her room. Sure, there'd been nights in the past that Felicia had flexed that "big girl" who "could take care of herself"-muscle by staying out, but most of those occurrences had been on the weekends. The few times those occurrences *hadn't* been on the weekends, however—occurrences when Dexter had been especially "riled up" with thoughts of, *She's probably out with some guy!*—she'd at least brought her books for the next day's classes.

Felicia's books still being in her room made her not being home especially worrisome for Dexter. Even more worrisome, however, was the irritating, almost itchy thought that there was a guy involved.

Though this slice of pie was the smallest, and though

it was absolutely buried in that same whipped topping of theory, Dexter found himself mulling over it the longest. It wasn't that it was the tastiest piece of truth-pie. Far from it. It was that it was the piece that fed Dexter's preferred narrative; the piece that pandered to how he *wanted* things to be. Not because Dexter necessarily *wanted* Felicia to be out there, *somewhere,* scared and alone save for the unwanted company of some brutish "Alpha" male with a penchant for shudder-inducing one-liners like, *"Hey, baby, looking for a good time?"* and *"Let me show you what I got!"* It was because Dexter relished in the idea that the day might come when Felicia and everyone else who'd demanded that he agree and respect their perspectives while shunning him for his would have to admit that they were wrong and that he was right.

It would also mean that the day had come when he would get to rescue her from such an encounter. And on that day—the day when Felicia would *finally* see him as more—he would...

Without meaning to, Dexter loosed a contented sigh.

He could all-but see the scene unfolding before him: Felicia tied up against her will—maybe even already stripped of all her clothes; her glorious breasts bulging past the unforgiving knots—and waiting in the dimmest corner of the no-doubt skeezy cellar. Her would-be attacker would be standing over her, preparing to do his worst, and that's when Dexter would make his move: bursting in at the last possible second and saving her from the deciding moment when her attacker was about to enter her. And...

Well, past that, Dexter wasn't sure. Not if he was being truthful with himself, at least.

Sure, he had a sizable collection of swords and knives and even guns. They adorned his walls and his shelves; cozied up or outright paired with his other collectibles and DVD boxsets, but, like everything else, they were all props and replicas. They weren't real. No more real than the Godzilla or King Kong statues in the kaiju shrine he kept next to his bookshelf. He'd had to confess that truth —*"No... it's not a real sword. None of them are real"*— when Felicia had interrupted him in the middle of showing off his new, five-foot-tall Rodan statue. And, though she'd done a good job of *pretending* to listen after that, he hadn't been able to escape the shame it had made him feel.

No, nothing in his makeshift "armory" was real. None of it was sharpened and none of it was loaded, and, still being truthful with himself, Dexter couldn't envision himself saving the day with any of what was hanging on his walls or resting on his shelves. Plastic, light-up laser swords and Sharpie-autographed prop guns from old sci-fi movies were awesome to display, but they'd quickly wind up very expensive garbage if he ever tried to wield them in combat. The most he could hope for from even his most prized firearm was a flashing muzzle and some faded sound effects.

Hardly the necessary firepower for a man on a mission to thwart a sexual assault.

Still... one couldn't be a hero if there wasn't first a situation that demanded heroism.

But did any of those bitter slices of pie leave Dexter feeling like the day for heroics had finally arrived?

Was it more likely that Felicia had gone out, perhaps on a date, gotten herself distracted, and then, forgetting about the next day and the necessary materials for it, decided to stay out?

I don't even want to think about how she might've gotten herself distracted, he thought with a sneer. *But...*

Yes. Absolutely. It was definitely possible, and it was definitely a more palatable slice from the truth-pie. Moreover, it demanded very little of that theory topping. But...

But...

But then Dexter would have to be ridiculous to worry, right?

Then he'd have to admit that Felicia and everyone else was right; that it was none of his business; that she *was* a "big girl" who "could take care of herself." Then, forced to admit all that, he'd have to admit that maybe his fixation *was* ridiculous and inappropriate.

"Fixation."

He hated that word. Same with "ridiculous" and "inappropriate." Those were words that always traveled alongside "fixation," and Dexter was tired of hearing them—especially from people like Felicia and her mother. They were the ones who'd been saying that his "fixation" was "ridiculous" and "inappropriate," and he knew they'd just as quickly say that it was his "ridiculous" and "inappropriate" "fixation" that had him visiting her room and looking around for clues regarding her whereabouts.

Well the joke's on them, isn't it? he thought.

Because it was then—while being "ridiculous" and "inappropriate"—that Dexter had discovered the required texts for that day's classes in Felicia's room. And it was because of that so-called "fixation" that he knew what books she'd be needing for that day's classes. All of which meant that Dexter was able to note Felicia's absence long before anybody else. In any other case, he supposed all of that would have people celebrating him as some sort of natural detective—*a modern-day Sherlock or maybe even a self-taught Batman!*—but, because he was Dexter and, as a result, never offered a single shred of respect, he already knew that his expert sleuthing would be lost on others.

After all, he seethed, *when you're me, giving a damn is a "fixation," and being committed is "ridiculous" and "inappropriate."*

Assholes!

As far as Dexter was concerned, it was everyone else who was ridiculous and inappropriate.

So when he broke the news to her mother that Felicia wasn't home and that her school books were still in her room, it came as little surprise when Karen said, "When will you stop obsessing over your sister's business?"

Because, yes, technically Felicia was his sister. Although, in Dexter's defense, she was only technically his *step*-sister. It hadn't been worth all the drama *before,* of course, but *now*—all thanks to Karen marrying Dexter's father—everyone had to act like he was some sort of degenerate for feeling the same feelings he had before.

"Not my fault that our parents getting married put her

in the bedroom across from mine," as he'd put it during one of his therapy sessions.

And it wasn't like Karen had done anything *except* ruin Dexter's life with the decision to marry his father. She hadn't saved the day by saying, *"I do,"* and she certainly hadn't stopped the cancer from killing her new husband only two years after the wedding. No, the only thing that had been accomplished was to force Dexter to accept that his longtime crush was suddenly *also* his sister.

So much for my perfect prom-fantasy, he'd lamented even during the ceremony five years earlier.

Then, with the loss of Daddy-dearest, he'd been thrown back into a single-parent household, only this time it had been with an emotionally vacant stepmother and her daughter, whom Dexter *still* couldn't stop lusting after.

And there was *nothing* wrong with that!

Hell, if the buzz surrounding PornHub was any indicator, *plenty* of step-siblings were pursuing their less-than-wholesome feelings towards one another. And, yeah, of course everyone was saying that those videos were fake and that the guys in them weren't really the girls' stepbrothers, but that was all for the sake of paperwork. Dexter saw how the couples in those videos looked at one another, and there was no faking *that*. It was how he'd been looking at Felicia, after all—not to mention how he'd dreamt of having Felicia look back at him—so he knew that it was real.

It had to be!

So long as the pornos were real, his hopes weren't in

vain. And, after saving Felicia from her would-be assailant—however he managed to do that—maybe she'd be willing to let him film the sex they'd have after...

Perhaps even right after saving her...

With her still all naked...

Still tied up...

Maybe—

"When will you stop obsessing over your sister's business?"

Emotionally vacant, as always.

A bright, scalding burn assaulted Dexter's cheeks. His jaw tightened, and his eyes dropped to the kitchen table until his still untouched bowl of Lucky Charms was all that occupied his vision. He fetched the spoon, scooped up a pile of milk-drenched marshmallows, and shoveled them into his mouth. As his jaw worked the mound of sweetness, he asked himself why he'd even bothered to bring up Felicia's absence to Karen.

Of course her mother wouldn't care.

She never cared.

Not about anything.

Most of the time she seemed to be waiting for the world to just burn away and take all the worrisome business with it.

And the rest of that is spent enjoying the aftermath of Dad's hearty insurance policy.

Not that the widow *needed* any more money. Even before Dexter's dad had died—long before she'd even married Dexter's dad and ruined Dexter's life, in fact—Karen had spent most of her time enjoying the perks of unearned wealth when she wasn't too busy resenting the world. Her own father had been some sort of tycoon, and the fortune he'd amassed had, of course, become hers. All that wealth had gone on in some way or another to spur yet even more wealth, all of it utterly undeserved as far as Dexter was concerned. Even more undeserved was the way that her net worth had grown that much further when Dexter's dad had died. Despite all that money, however, Karen hadn't been the least bit interested in helping Felicia or Dexter further their education at any sort of reputable school. Hell, the misery-pumping, money-grubbing bitch couldn't even be bothered to splurge on either of her "darling children" to stay on campus in the Kenwood Community College dorms!

And why would she? Dexter thought, still mashing away at his Lucky Charms. *She probably expects me and Felicia to burn away with the rest of the world when the day comes.*

Of course she didn't take his concern seriously.

Of course she spurned him for even bringing it up.

It was just whiny ol' Dexter being "ridiculous" and "inappropriate."

Too bad for Karen, though, because Dexter had noticed her little slipup. It hadn't been much—just the slightest twitch in her lip when he'd mentioned that Felicia wasn't home—but he'd seen it. It was too subtle to be called a smile, but there'd definitely been something there.

It was a break in an otherwise ongoing haze of disconnection and disinterest, one that she hadn't had to spend a small fortune to achieve.

And he'd seen it!

He was sure of it!

Dexter, if only to keep himself from smiling at that, filled his mouth with more oats and sugar. Then, still staring at his once-more emotionally vacant stepmother, he smacked away at the wad and decided once-and-for-all that—*no*—he wasn't being ridiculous or inappropriate.

Karen knew something!

And Dexter was going to find out what.

CHAPTER 2
NOT THAT ANYONE WAS ASKING...

Not that anyone was asking—not that anyone was around to ask—but Varian, if asked, thought he'd likely say that he'd had better nights. He'd had worse, sure; far, *far* worse. He more considered himself a connoisseur on shitty nights—*and days*—than he'd even dare to consider himself a leader to his crew. Granted, he'd never tell them that. It sort of deflated the whole "leader"-thing if the leader in question turned around and said, *"You know what? I know fuck-all about what I'm doing! You'd all likely fare better if you threw me into the nearest torture pit and forgot all about me."* Then again, if anybody in his crew actually knew about what he was—what he'd *been*—and just how bad those "worse" nights had gotten, they'd either run as far and as fast from him as they could, laugh themselves to death, or just outright murder him and be done with it. If he thought long enough on it, he could even tell which of those any one of his crew would likely opt for. He didn't have time to think on it, and, truth-be-told, he was already lying to himself: even *if* anyone was around to ask he wouldn't admit to having worst nights. He'd likely just shrug and, at best, offer up something like, *"Hell's a shit-place. It'd be foolish to expect anything other than shitty circumstances."*

But, again, nobody was around to ask.

It was just Varian, alone with a heart full of shame and confusion, a mouth full of blood, and a mind overflowing with rage.

"Th-that's... ***MINE!***" he growled, spitting out the word with a wad of crimson and dragging himself from the floor.

He stood, felt something inside of him—something broken—disagree with its new angle against his guts. He growled again, gritted his teeth, and drove his fist into his own chest. That broken thing broke a little more, disagreed a little louder, and raked angrily against one of his organs.

It was an old-albeit-familiar sensation; for a moment he was back in those old, worse nights. He lied to himself, said it was fine—*But is it ever?*—and spit again. There was no blood in it this time, but he wasn't fond of the flavor that last word—"***MINE!***"—left in his mouth. He'd only been thinking it, only been *feeling* it, for—what?—a few hours. *Maybe.* Probably not even that long, though. It hadn't even been happening long enough to feel like a habit yet, but already it was feeling old.

"Not gonna happen," he muttered to himself.

It seemed to answer an unasked question, even if only to himself.

After all, nobody was around to ask.

Not *yet,* at least. Varian suspected that the noise had woken the others. It must have. If they could sleep through a fucking tentacled wrecking ball of a demon demolishing the front half of their building then he might have to pick between running as far and as fast from them as he could, laughing himself to death, or just outright murdering the lot and being done with it. Then again, the demolition *had* only just gone down—their most recent prize had only *just* been snatched up and hauled off—and maybe expecting an instant response was being a tad unfair.

Yeah, Varian was sure they were already in the process of getting from *there* to *here.* Unfortunately, his crew was either asleep or in the process of trying to get there, and he didn't have the time for any of them to find their assholes let alone their armaments.

Then Varian was moving; hauling up and over the pile of rubble that was blocking his path and landing in the night-bathed streets of Hell. That broken thing inside him gave a little twist and poked something that felt important. Varian pounded the area harder, figuring if he broke whatever the broken thing was a bit more then there wouldn't be enough left to stab his insides. It was just a matter of enduring the agony for the time being. Whatever it was and whatever it was perforating on its little adventure inside of him could grow back in time.

"Can't grow back everything," an all-too-familiar feminine voice chimed in the back of his skull, punctuating the reminder with a coo and a chuckle.

Varian punched the broken thing again. This time he felt it pass through one of his lungs.

He'd still had worse nights, but this one seemed to be eager to put itself in the running.

"Where in the realms did...?" he began, but trailed off when he heard a muffled scream climb over the rooftops a few blocks over.

Then he was moving again.

His two legs carried him as fast as they could.

It wasn't fast enough.

It never would be.

Not for Varian.

He wanted to tell himself that he was built for better things—that he *should* be built for better things—but even then, even in those worse days, it was tough to convince even himself that any of what he was doing was "better things."

Just better at it, he thought with a growl as he launched himself in a single bound from the street and onto the bowed metal roof of a street vendor selling fried shit-viper. The demon beneath him snarled out something in the old tongue, but Varian was already using his new foothold to push off yet again and missed most of what was said. As he scrambled to secure his hold on the neighboring building and begin his climb he added, ***A lot better!***

He scuttled up the side of the structure, his remaining hands and feet effortlessly finding miniscule grips and footholds. With the din of the streets growing distant behind him, a sort of alien non-silence took over. There was no such thing as absolute silence in Hell—none that Varian had ever known, at least—but there was this beautifully twisted realm of gray where noise seemed so irrelevant that one could almost—*almost!*—will it into nonexistence. There was still plenty of noise spiraling up from the streets. There would never *not* be noise, no matter how early or late it was. The noise, however, was of such little consequence to Varian at that moment that he could listen past it; listen for...

THERE!

The muffled, swaying pitch of the breeder's screams.

The wrecking ball had changed directions. That, or it had taken a wrong turn and been forced to backtrack at some point. Either way, it hadn't put any new distance between itself and Varian—it had only set itself an equal distance away in the other direction.

"Big motherfucker like that," Varian muttered to himself, flinging himself the rest of the way up the wall and landing in mid-sprint on the rooftop, "isn't made to navigate a city like this." This demanded the question, *Then why come here at all?* But Varian, even as he scrambled to crest the upward angle of the roof and started down the embankment at the other side, could answer that much:

Because she was a *breeder!*

She was a fresh piece of human pussy: no teeth or barbs, no scales, and no acidic mucus. A warm orifice that wasn't liable to maim, murder, or mutilate anybody foolish enough to get too close. Sure, not just anybody could *breed* with a breeder, but most in Hell were starved for a female who would *willingly* open herself up to them. Then again, "willingly" only representing a marginal hurdle when a bit of torture was involved. This *was* Hell, after all.

And there's always a catch in Hell!

If a breeder didn't give itself up on the first pass, there wasn't a devil or demon in any of the seven realms that wasn't willing to put in the time to "convince" them. Varian sneered at the thought; realized that, yup, he *could* hate Hell and its denizens more than he already did.

But at least it made them predictable. Every last filthy, wretched, scum-sucking fucking one of them!

And, really, wasn't that why Varian wanted the breeder in the first place? Because wasn't taking the Hell king's prized "army factory" a surefire way to get him angry? Because wasn't anger a great way to motivate stupidity in an enemy, *especially* when that enemy was the eternal, take-three-realms-by-force warmonger, Asmorias? This was an inconvenience, sure, and a painful one at that, but wasn't a demon of *that* size going through all the trouble of dragging its fat ass through the unaccommodating confines of this city *proof* that Varian and his crew had stolen something of value?

Then again, if a demon of *that* size even made an attempt at the breeder, Varian doubted she'd be much good to anybody anymore.

Bad enough she got busy with Shik, he thought, wondering just how much "value" was lost anytime somebody decided to get their dick wet with her. *But if her pussy can stretch across the whole of Hell then Asmorias is going to take it as an act of war.* And, sure, the devil might not have his army of perfect heirs to set out against the four realms he wasn't ruling, but he hadn't needed a bred legion to take another two realms when he'd decided the one he ruled over wasn't enough.

That thought and the question that followed was nearly enough to give Varian pause; nearly enough to spill him over the edge of the rooftop as he braced to leap to the next one.

Had Asmorias needed an army of heirs to get where he did?

And, if he *hadn't,* then why had he stopped at the three? It didn't take a genius to know that, with each new realm conquered, Asmorias claimed that much more power. So why, with all that gained power, would he have stopped?

Unless he exhausted the resources he'd used to conquer the other two realms, Varian thought.

Resources... like a specially-bred army.

If he'd been back home—back in his room or back in his chair—Varian might have started beating himself up for not having thought of this sooner. It was still only a guess, a theory, but not an entirely unreasonable one. If somebody was there to ask, he guessed he'd be able to talk at great lengths about why it was perfectly feasible.

But nobody was around to ask.

Again, Varian found himself furious and demanding to himself where the others were, then just as quickly reminding himself that it was unfair to think that way. The chaos that the others would be discovering back at the base was bad enough that they could spend the entirety of the night thinking over it and never once consider actually *leaving* to see what might have spilled into the streets. He imagined Norya frantically—and futilely—digging through the piles of stone for either him or the breeder; could imagine the others adding to the effort, calling out or sniffing around. And even *if* one of them thought enough to step out into the hubbub of the city, it wasn't like they knew what to look for.

Best hope I've got for backup is if Shik starts sniffing after the breeder, he thought. And, yeah, that was a perfectly reasonable—if not outright highly likely—thing for the scrappy pussy-hound to do. Then again, Varian knew how panic always managed to get in the way. If Shik was afraid that he or the breeder had been buried in the rubble, he might never even think to aim his prowess for crotch-sniffing towards the rest of the city.

Like it or not...

Varian's whirlwind of thoughts hiccupped, and, with it, so did his body. He was in mid-leap, coming down on a particularly steep roof slated with dragon scales, when the raw, savage wave of *her* collided with his senses.

The smell—the *entirety!*—of the breeder was like crashing into a slate wall.

Nostrils flared.

Muscles seized.

Varian's entire body thrummed with a single-yet-echoing chant of **MINE!**

He didn't so much land on the roof as he crashed feet-first on it. He absently imagined Shik offering that "feet-first" *was* a landing, but could just as easily imagine Kaishu arguing that the only true landing *was* a true landing. *This* was not a true landing. Varian's feet felt the rooftop, told the rest of him too late that they'd made contact, and his legs folded before he could tell them *not* to.

Then he was tumbling and thinking, *If only I had four...*

Scales the size of his palm came unhinged and began to slide in angled rows towards the edge of the roof. The shimmering avalanche threatened to drag the still-tumbling Varian over, and he had to aim himself in mid-fall to keep from getting dumped back into the streets.

Her! his mind swam, still soaking in the smell of the breeder. **MINE!**

"Shut... up!" Varian heard him grunt at himself—was he actually *talking* to that accursed thought now?—and he worked to complete the sloppy somersault while half-crawling up the roof, using his hands to steer his flailing body while working to get his feet under him.

But if the smell was this strong...

"... *close.*"

He wasn't sure if he'd said it or thought it, but the fact —because it was an undeniable fact: the breeder *was* close!—somehow gave him the necessary burst that he needed to slip past the collapsing shingles. Then, back on his feet, his legs folded like a set of springs eager to test themselves...

And he jumped.

It was as blind as it was reckless, and Varian caught himself wondering how two lonely legs could push him so far. This, however, was a distant thought in a darkened part of his brain; a part where rationality and logic and reason dwelled. Typically driven by rationality and logic and reason, Varian might have found this "darkening" to be worth a moment-or-two of concern, but that would have been the rational thing to do; the logical and reasonable thing to do.

Varian didn't offer a moment-or-two of thought on the blind, reckless leap. Instead, still in midair—now in mid-fall—he roared. It was a sound he hadn't made in a long time, a sound he'd admittedly let himself forget, and it hit his ears with a strange, savage sort of nostalgia.

"MINE!"

That last part struck that darkened part of his mind as cringeworthy, and if anyone had been around to ask, Varian would insist that the roar was the only sound he'd made as he came down on the wrecking ball who'd stolen what he'd worked so hard to steal in the first place.

Not that anyone was asking…

CHAPTER 3
BOOM! CLAP!
THE SOUND OF MY HEART...

Not that anyone was asking—not that anyone was around to ask—but Felicia, if asked, thought that she'd likely not be lying if she'd said she'd never had a worse night. Then again, having no memory beyond the past few hours and having had a big chunk of those few hours occupied by raging arousal and orgasmic bliss, it was tough to say how any of it stacked against other nights she'd had. She couldn't exactly consider herself an expert on bad nights, but she had to imagine *this* was something of a scale-tipper.

This, of course, being...

What?

Godzilla? A kaiju?

Both words passed through her mind, instantly meant nothing, and left her in more agony than she was already in. This, however, wasn't saying much. She'd been drop-dead tired and sore-as-Hell *before* all of *this; before* her little spat with Varian-the-living-flame.

Varian...

Felicia wasn't even sure if he was still alive. Worse yet, she wasn't even sure why she cared. The things he'd said to her...

"... he means to use you—well, your pussy, really; the rest of you just keeps the baby-making parts alive and running—to make an army; to just consistently pump out soldier-after-soldier..."

She *wanted* to hate him for what he'd said, but...

But was it his fault that he told an ugly truth?

He hadn't had to be such a raging dick about it, sure, but did it change that, deep down, every syllable of it had rung within Felicia as some sort of cosmic truth. Varian had literally mapped out the details of her situation, the WHY behind her waking up in Hell and feeling the way she felt, and, even if he hadn't tried to soften the impact of it—even if he'd said it all to hurt her—it didn't make any of it any less true. And...

"And he'll wipe out entire cities—slaughter anybody —just to claim the entirety of Hell."

Those were not the concerns of a horrible person...

"But Hell's just the beginning, breeder."

They weren't the worries of a selfish, uncaring man...

"... he'll use his monopoly on Hell to flood into other worlds; climb across them like rungs on a fucking ladder."

They were the concerns of somebody bold...

"... he'll take Heaven, and he'll burn it so completely that the only light left in the cosmos will be the wretched embers of Hell; his Hell."

They were the concerns of somebody *desperate*...

"His and yours, breeder, because the endless current of spawn will be marching out of your cunt."

Somebody who saw her as nothing but a weapon to be fired at...

At *EVERYTHING!*

"That's *why I hate you...*"

"*... because keeping your hungry womb away from the Hell king is the only way of keeping* all of that *from becoming a reality.*"

And, really, did any of *that* make Varian a bad guy? A dick, maybe—even Norya had outright confessed that he *was* that—but...

"*So I will suffer the annoyance of your existence—roll my eyes and fight to ignore the stink of tailored cunt—solely because I know that you being here is* ruining *Asmorias' plans.*"

So badly...

Felicia wanted to hate Varian so very, very badly, but, despite this, she couldn't help but worry about him. The monster—this *thing*—had come right through a wall; it had gone through the side of a building as if it was nothing. She'd thought it had to be some sort of machine, but what had come through was a giant demon. It was so big, in fact, that it was very clearly having trouble just *carrying* her through the city; its gigantic, wavering body knocking this-and-that as it struggled to navigate between the buildings. To see something like *that* absently strike Varian—to see his limp, ragdoll-like body fly through the air and hit the wall as hard as he had—made it damn-near impossible to hold onto any hope that he might have survived.

This, and the stifling, crushing weight of the massive tentacle wrapped around her body, forced another scream from her. The slimy, wriggling nub that the tentacle ended in had long-since capped itself over her mouth—the thick, squelching limb nearly suffocating her entirely each time it slipped over her nostrils—and this made her screams all-but inaudible even to herself. She'd dared to bite the thing moments after it first stifled her, but it did nothing to budge the blockage; it only motivated the rest of the terrible limb to squeeze her that much harder. All the same, much as it hurt and made breathing that much harder, rage and panic were powerful motivators. The screams came, again and again.

CEASE, QUEEN, LEST THE VERMIN AND DEGENERATES VENTURE TO EMBOLDEN THEMSELVES!

Felicia's life, as she'd come to know it in the past few hours, had known only one consistence: headaches. At that point, she more considered herself a connoisseur of head-pain more than she'd even dare to consider herself a person. If, in his long-winded rant regarding the vile nature of her existence, Varian had come out and said that Felicia was nothing more than a headache that had been given a body, she'd likely have believed that just as thoroughly as she believed—*knew!*—the rest of what he'd said.

This headache, however, came with a lot more words than the others, and it took an embarrassingly long moment before she realized that *this* headache was actually the *thing* that had taken her *talking* to her. It's speech —*Thankfully!* she supposed—was not spoken aloud, but, rather, run in her head; echoing in her mind. Much as it hurt, though, she felt certain that anything *spoken* by something so large, especially with her so close, would mean a much, *much* larger headache.

Felicia craned her head to try to get a look at the thing. Though her angle was awkward, the thing's tentacled grip not allowing for much movement one way or the other, she caught sight of a head roughly as tall as her entire body occupied by a series of jagged "cuts" that seemed to be its eyes. This, however, was based on a hazy view from the outermost edges of her periphery, she realized, and those "cuts," she supposed, could just as easily be mouths. This thought made her all the more thankful that it hadn't spoken aloud to her.

She garbled out something that *barely* sounded like *"Let me go!"* and, halfway through another mess of noise that *might* have been *"Where are you taking me?"* the tentacle began shaking her. The shaking, which twisted her away even further and stole that partial, peripheral view she had of the thing, only stopped when the last mess of *"... taking me?"* fell silent.

WE ARE RETURNING, QUEEN! the thing thought-said to her, and Felicia was filled with questions as she realized that she could "hear" pride in this strange sort of not-voice. *KING ASMORIAS DEMANDS—*

At the mention of the Hell king's name, Felicia loosed a fresh batch of screams.

The giant tentacle shook her. Harder.

I'LL REFER YOU TO MY PRIOR REQUEST, QUEEN: CEASE! it demanded, then, its not-tone dropping to one of annoyance, it added, *YOU SMELL OF HER, BUT NEVER IN ALL HER CENTURIES HAS SHE TROUBLED ME SO!*

Still stifled, Felicia groaned a lame parody of *"Smell of who? Who the fuck are you talking about?"* into the sticky depths of the tentacle.

The thing shook her again, but answered all the same, *ISADORA:* ***THE PRINCESS!***

Felicia's head was swimming in agony and confusion. How could there already be a princess if this *thing* insisted on calling her "queen?" She barked a nonsensical question into the tentacle, this one not even bearing any resemblance to true words.

Somehow, however, the *thing* seemed to understand all the same and began to answer all the same with, *ONE OF* ***THE TWELVE****; ONE OF SIX I GUARD. OF THEM,* ***THE PRINCESS****—*

Whatever strange, headachey rant the *thing* had planned was interrupted then by a carnal sound—something intimidating enough to stop not only the *thing's* not-words, but also its giant, staggering steps. Felicia felt herself tilt as the tentacle that held her did the same; the whole of the *thing's* body shifting and aiming itself upwards; aiming itself in the direction of the sound. Then...

"MINE!"

Then...

BOOM!
CLAP!

The sound of my heart...?

Felicia wasn't sure what she was hearing, but the resulting impact a moment later had her caring less about what she'd heard and more about what she was going to do about the tentacle—the tentacle that had been crushing her and suffocating her, sure, but the same tentacle that was holding her at a dizzying height over the city—as it started to loosen its grip on her. Blind to whatever was happening, she could only stare out at that strange night sky and its multiple moons as she heard several meaty *THUD*s sound behind her. The tentacle's grasp around her slackened that much more. The slimy nub over her mouth trembled, tightened to a point where she began to worry that her skull might not survive the ordeal, and then fell away. She gasped, regretted it as she sucked in a wad of *something,* and then screamed.

The tentacle had fallen away from her entirely.

She was dropping.

Then she wasn't.

And then she was again.

Her scream had been knocked into airy silence in the brief in-between. Whatever had stopped her initial fall—caught her?—had winded her in the process. With a sort of stunned, reflective sliver of memory, she realized only after she'd started falling again that the *whatever* in question had been Varian, and that the "stopping" hadn't so much been him *catching* her so much as it had been him slamming into a neighboring building—his outstretched limbs momentarily snagging her in mid-descent—and her sliding off of him and back into a freefall. Then, unable to summon a new scream in time, Felicia heard that same carnal sound behind—*above?*—her, and another, much heavier *THUD*.

Beside her, the towering body of the *thing* that had taken her shuddered and began to sink. Seeming to defy the rest of its form, the tentacle that had been holding her

—the tentacle that had fallen away a moment earlier and plunged her into this moment—rose to catch itself on the same building that Varian had just struck. In that instant, Felicia's midsection caught the slime-drenched appendage, and she half-slid and half-rolled over its length before colliding with the *thing's* body.

It was like being thrown straight into the ground with nothing but the grass to soften the impact. The entirety of the *thing's* body seemed to be hard, unforgiving muscle beneath a slime-covered veil of veiny, throbbing flesh. She had just enough time to think *It's a giant, tentacled slug!* before another of those headaches struck her with the same ferocity that she'd struck the *thing's* side. Then, with a grotesque series of wet *pop*s, the slimy sheen that had held her in that instant began to relinquish her body back to gravity...

Then, once more, she was dropping.

"I gotcha, doll!" a blessedly familiar voice sang, and suddenly Felicia *wasn't* dropping anymore.

Norya!

Felicia might have called her an angel if it wasn't for all the evidence to the contrary.

Then her feet were on the ground, and Felicia couldn't imagine ever feeling more relieved to be standing.

"Zaiden," the towering she-demon called out, "get her someplace safe!"

"I can take her!" Shik trumpeted, already taking her by the wrist and getting as far as "Come on, baby. We don't wanna hang around—" before a giant hand caught his opposite shoulder.

"No," Norya said. Her yellow eyes were already starting back in the direction of the giant demon, and Felicia thought she caught a glimmer of worry in them as she did. "I need you with me," she told Shik without looking away, "and she'll be safer with Zaiden."

"All due respect, ma'am," a low, even voice rumbled, and Felicia loosed a small yelp as she realized that stoic soldier-demon was standing only a few feet away, "but don't you think I'm better equipped to assist you in—"

"I've already asked you to cut it out with that 'ma'am'-stuff, Zai," Norya interrupted with a sigh. "And, yeah, I think you're better equipped than Shik in *a lot* of ways, but—"

"HEY!" Shik shot from beside Felicia.

Norya, either not hearing the orange demon's whining or not caring, went on addressing Zaiden: "—I *know* that she'll be safe with you. Shik's likely to buckle in an instant and try to—"

"You think I can't keep it in my pants when *death's* on my heels?" Shik demanded, finally letting go of Felicia.

"I wouldn't trust you to keep it in your pants if you were on your deathbed," Norya chided. "With a breeder by your side, though, I doubt even death would keep your dick down." Those yellow eyes slunk down to take in Felicia, and she was startled to see the giant she-demon's cheeks go pink. "Even I couldn't resist the effe—"

It was Zaiden's rifle that interrupted this time. The teeth-rattling report echoed between the surrounding buildings, and a sharp chirp of pain sounded from above. The ground trembled as the giant demon staggered back, colliding with something tall and unforgiving the next block over. Felicia heard a few startled cries and shouts of warning before the increasingly familiar sound of a collapsing building drowned them out. Zaiden snarled around another round of gunfire, his face a mask of determination and desperation. No sooner had his finger eased off the trigger than he was firing more words in Norya's direction:

"I'M NOT GOING TO LEAVE YOU TO HANDLE *THAT* WITHOUT—"

"I'm *ordering* you to take the breeder away from here," Norya said, her voice dipping into an unnervingly calm and diplomatic tone.

With no way of knowing, Felicia knew that she'd just won the argument. *And she barely spoke over a whisper to do it,* she marveled.

Zaiden's face twisted in the next moment. It looked like he was in pain—like Norya's low, simple words had actually penetrated him—but he fought through it to utter a defeated, "Ma'am... yes, ma'am." Then, wincing at a sudden thought, he cast a nervous glance in Felicia's direction before lifting himself on his toes in a wasted effort to close the distance between him and the she-demon. "But what if I succumb to the...?" he asked, unable to finish the question.

Norya, already hoisting a squirming Shik off his feet, offered the soldier-demon a shrug. "I suspect you will succumb, Zai. I just expect you to have her somewhere safe before you do." Then, leaning in to give him a kiss between his long, spiraling horns, she set the side of her giant palm against his face and said, "And I expect you to be every bit the gentleman with her that you always are with me."

A sheepish grin crested Zaiden's face at that, and he gave a single nod.

It was a simple gesture, but it was enough to have Norya looking reassured. Nodding back, she rose to her full height with Shik now perched on her shoulder.

"Don't forget me, baby," the orange demon called after Felicia, punctuating the request with an air-kiss and a wagging tongue between two fingers.

Then they were running: Norya stampeding towards the mayhem and Zaiden scooping up Felicia and rolling free of a swinging tentacle as it swooped in to reclaim her. His boots kicked up a bit of trash as they rocketed them away from the massive, oozing limb. Caught off guard by his speed, she yelped again and buried herself deeper against the soldier-demon's chest.

Though he seemed otherwise unwavering, she thought she felt the slightest tremor under her palms as she did.

It had a similar tremor creeping through her own chest, and she felt her nipples pucker against—

Because of-fucking-course I am! she thought as the realization that, save for the ridiculously oversized robe she'd borrowed from Norya, she was still naked as she was being carried off by yet another demon.

CHAPTER 4
AT EASE, SOLDIER

Norya had said that Felicia would be safer with Zaiden. She had also said that Zaiden would make it farther before—*"But what if I succumb to the...?"*—needing to stop. To Norya's credit, she'd been right.

On both accounts.

Unfortunately, as it turned out, Zaiden wasn't safer with Felicia, and Felicia absolutely *could not* make it as far as her demon escort before the scalding heat under her flesh started to become too much.

She suspected she'd still managed to last longer than Shik would have managed, but not by much. She couldn't be certain just how much longer she'd lasted, however, because Zaiden had only carried her half-a-block—coming to an intersection where the alley they'd been fleeing fed into a street that had become a raging river of fleeing demon bodies—before she'd lost all sense of focus. Time and distance became laughably irrelevant as her heaving chest and dripping pussy screamed for attention.

HELLISH ASCENT

She remembered thinking, *Holy hell! Really?* before the hilarity of it had her giggling around her stuttering moans and she began making mad grabs for Zaiden's crotch.

"M-Miss, you're not—*mph!*—making this easy," he'd tried, swatting her attempts away with one hand while, with the other, swinging his rifle in the direction of a trio of demons who'd spun around in response to Felicia's rampaging breeder pheromones.

In hindsight, she suspected that her calls of *"FUCK ME!"* were just as likely an attention-getter in that instant.

The trio of demons had backed off at the sight of Zaiden's rifle leveling itself in their direction. Unfortunately, another demon—one with a gun of his very own—saw the weapon as an invitation to compete for the desperate breeder, and the challenge had been accepted without words. A gentle *click* of the new weapon being cocked behind him was all the warning the soldier-demon was offered.

It had been enough.

Almost.

The shock to Felicia's already spiraling senses—her flushed skin and wavering sense of up-and-down—had her mind clearing a second later. They were falling. The screaming horniness in her head scattered from a far heavier, looming thought—*Not again!*—and then she'd landed with an airy grunt. It hadn't hurt, not as much as it should have, but that was only because Zaiden had managed to put himself under her before he'd hit the street.

Felicia heard him hiss in pain. She heard him curse in a language she shouldn't have been able to understand but somehow did. Then she heard Zaiden's rifle bark out a single shot. Behind her, she heard the demon who'd shot at them gasp and whimper, but the sound of a his body hitting the street had been swallowed by another's shout:

"SHE'S A BREEDER!"

As it turned out, the demon trio that Zaiden had scared off with his rifle had been part of a minority, because it seemed in the next moment that most of the demons occupying that street were armed.

Any lingering horniness still swimming in Felicia's head found itself dry and disinterested as a storm of gunfire began, and Norya's claims to her ongoing safety were put to the test.

Seeing dozens of demons taking aim at him, Zaiden had lunged for fallen demon he'd just shot. The first shot was faster, but not by much. A second later, draped in a shield of dead demon meat, the soldier had pulled Felicia to her feet. She remembered gasping at his strength as he did, but only because it had choked the scream that wanted to follow immediately after.

Her savior had been shot!

Twice!

She could only imagine that one of the bullet wounds had been from the shot that was slightly faster than its target, but that left her to wonder which of the many shots that had already been fired were responsible for the second. In either case, in only a few short seconds, her brave soldier-demon escort—who *had,* true to Norya's claims, kept her safe and resisted her breeder pull—had found himself with a bullet in his right calf and a long, angry gash across the side of his jaw where a bullet had grazed him.

She'd started to say, "YOU'VE BEEN SHOT!" but—*Thank God!*—he'd shouted over this:

"MOVE IT!"

Though they were far more mindful in that moment than what she'd been about to say, they'd wound up just as useless. Before Felicia could even begin to remember how to use her legs, Zaiden was using his own for the both of them.

The dead demon he'd been shielding them with was airborne, hurled somewhere in between his ultimately useless words and his suddenly freed hands hoisting her up once more. From over his shoulder, she watched the corpse corkscrew towards the crowd, its arms and legs flailing in all directions as it came down, and bowled over several of the ones nearest to the front. A wave of curses burped up in the calamity, intermingling with a series of shouts to the others to stop shooting out of concern that a stray shot might hit their prize. Despite this, a few more shots *ping*ed off the street, chasing Zaiden's pumping legs.

Felicia imagined the ones still shooting were trying to stagger him all over again, but, as the injury to his leg didn't seem to be enough to stop him, she couldn't muster the worry that anything else would.

Once more proving Norya's claims regarding her safety, the soldier-demon had managed to get them away.

The moment he had, however, was the moment that he'd finally started to succumb...

... to the bullet in his calf.

Hobbling another block-and-a-half, he'd finally steered them towards a boarded up cellar door set into the side of a building. Felicia couldn't be sure what it was for, but doubt or concern did nothing to keep Zaiden from breaking through the chain of link-beetles holding it shut and ushering her inside. As they slipped past the threshold and started down the steps, the full weight of what had just transpired came cycling back and dragged a startled sob from Felicia's throat.

"Are you alright?" Zaiden asked as he pulled the cellar door shut behind them.

The sudden darkness that followed was enough to keep her from answering. She didn't want to risk alerting any of the infinite nightmarish possibilities of what might be surrounding them to their presence. Imagining such things, she nearly screamed when she spotted two glowing orbs swaying to-and-fro only a short distance behind her, but then Zaiden pulled the cord to an overhead lamp and revealed them to be his own eyes.

His own tired, pain-laced eyes.

They were so blue that they almost threatened the realm of purple. Felicia distantly thought, *Navy blue,* and then found herself having to stifle another giggle at the surreal obviousness of that fact. *Because* of-fucking-course *the soldier-demon would have—*

"Well...?" he said, and Felicia saw then that those tired, pain-laced eyes were *also* filled with worry.

Remembering his yet unanswered question—*"Are*

you alright?"—she offered a sheepish nod before following it up with, "Thanks to you."

No sooner was it past her lips than she felt ridiculous for saying it.

Any awkward nerve that her words might have struck went unphased in the soldier-demon, though. If anything, he didn't seem to have heard Felicia's words; only registered them as an extension of her nod. She watched his nervous, wandering gaze slow in its relentless prowling over her body, then, with it, the rest of his body began to relax. He let out a heavy sigh that threatened to become a growl...

And then he staggered.

Zaiden cursed and fought to regain his footing, only to overbalance and topple into a shelf littered with cans and spare parts. The ensuing clangs and tolls of loose metal had both of them flinching. Felicia only barked out a nervous gasp, but Zaiden snarled and was halfway through leveling his rifle before he realized there was nobody there. Once again, the process of relaxing seemed to take more out of him than he had to give. Managing not to stagger again, he dragged himself to a support beam, leaned his back against it, and let gravity drag him onto his rump. A cloud of dust kicked up beneath him at the same moment he was drawing in a heavy breath, and a coughing fit ensued.

Felicia, watching, chewed her lip. Without realizing it, she'd begun reaching for him. A nagging cramp in her shoulder told her that her arm had been outstretched longer than she'd have suspected. Despite this, she didn't lower it. Instead, she followed the effort: walking in the direction of her empty, grasping hand.

She thought, *Like a dog dragging on a leash,* and then felt the already familiar pang of agony in the back of her mind.

It seemed to ask, *WHAT IS "DOG"?*

It seemed to ask, *WHAT IS "LEASH"?*

And it outright demanded to know why a breeder—a creature made solely to serve in Hell—should know of such things.

Felicia didn't have any answers. She didn't even have any clues. She thought on those taboo, triggering words—*"dog"* and *"leash;"* thought of them *together*—and was once more rewarded with pain and confusion. On their own though...

"FUCK ME LIKE A DOG!"
"PUT THE LEASH ON ME, DADDY!"

Ah, yes! The corner of Felicia's brain that was all-too-quick to punish her for thinking alien thoughts *loved* that. Though the words had no context together—*No reason why I should be thinking,* 'Like a dog dragging on a leash'—it seemed that, on their own, she could not only understand the words, she could think them without that infernal pain crashing over her.

ESPECIALLY if it guaranteed breeding!

That part of her brain—*The part that knows* EXACTLY *what I am and what I'm made for*—rewarded her for those thoughts. No sooner had that part thought, ***"FUCK ME LIKE A DOG!"*** and, ***"PUT THE LEASH ON ME, DADDY!"*** than Felicia's headache had vanished and been replaced with waves of rippling pleasure. She felt hot; felt like she was burning. All at once, she felt like that too-big robe she was wearing was too much.

"Felicia?"

She heard her name—heard it uttered in the soldier-demon's low, rumbling voice—and she heard herself moan in response. She thought, *"Say it into my pussy,"* and then wondered if she'd only thought it. She could almost taste the words, worried then that she might've just spoken them—*Fucking hope I did!*—and then she caught herself wanting to taste more. She thought, *Made for this,* and then she thought again, "Fuck me like a dog!"

This time, she *knew* she'd spoken aloud, but she couldn't bring herself to even pretend to be worried.

She heard Zaiden say her name again—heard it closer than before—then she heard him cough again.

"Z-Zai—" she began, blinking against the haze and realizing that she'd crossed the distance and was kneeling in front of him, "—den?"

Felicia could see that the soldier-demon was trembling. His greenish skin of his face was darkening; the yellow patches adorning his jaw starting to look more orange. He looked hot.

In every sense of the word... Felicia thought, realizing that she'd begun reaching for him again.

"A-are... are you... a-alright?" Zaiden asked her again, but he seemed to be struggling to make the words come out right.

Felicia wanted to answer him again, but she was

beyond making any words come out. She crawled nearer, hand-over-hand—***Like a dog! I'll crawl to you like one if you'll fuck me like one!***—and yelped as he loosed a seething hiss of pain.

Her palm had landed on his injured calf.

Zaiden yanked his leg away, teeth clenched and holding back the last of his agonized groan. The effort must have dislodged a remnant of the dusty air he'd been choking on, because he coughed again in the next instant.

A fresh trail of blood oozed from the cut on his cheek. Unsure of what she intended to do, she was already reaching for—

Blood.

There was more of it on her palm...

From his leg, she reminded herself.

She wanted to—**FUCK ME!**—check the wound.

She *needed* to—**FUCK ME LIKE A DOG!**—make sure that he was...

"A-are... are you... a-alright?"

Felicia tried to answer; tried to apologize. She thought that maybe she'd managed to get the words out, but she was swimming against a current of arousal. She wanted to say and do the right things, but that damnable haze had her unsure of everything.

She heard herself say, "Take your pants off," and told herself it was so that she could examine the gunshot to his calf.

Zaiden grumbled a halfhearted, "I-it's fine. *I'm* fine," but, even as he did, his hands were moving down; his shaking fingers fumbling with his belt's buckle. The look in his face seemed to say that he was telling himself he was doing it for the right reasons, too, but the throbbing bulge just below his working hands spoke louder.

Nothing, however, was louder than the breeder-part of Felicia's mind. It screamed again, ***"FUCK ME LIKE A DOG!"*** and this time she knew she'd said it out loud.

Then Zaiden's hands, still shaking, were on her. She gasped at the contact, screamed as his grip tightened—*God! I'm already cumming from his touch!*—and it wasn't until her panting moans subsided that Felicia realized that the soldier-demon's hold was holding her back. She whimpered, writhing, and felt the lingering waves of her orgasm crash against the jagged rocks of shame. Each pass seemed to whisper to her:

You're out of control!
This is all you'll ever be!
You're nothing but a whore now!

And, dirty as it made her feel, each of these whispers triggered another and yet another tiny climax in her. She groaned, leaned into Zaiden's hold, and repeated, "Fuck me!"

"I... I *can't!*" Zaiden croaked, staring back at her with a face that looked every bit as savage and strained as when he'd been fighting back in the streets. "N-Norya..." he moaned around the name—seemed to suffer his own small, shame-fueled orgasm as a result of saying it—and Felicia felt a ray of clarity punch through the horny storm clouds of her mind as he said, "Sh-she told me... keep you safe. *Ordered* me to—" he began, only to have another shuddering whimper cut him off.

Him and Norya...? Felicia thought, drawing back...

... but only slightly.

"You and Norya...?" she echoed aloud.

Hearing the name had Zaiden shuddering again; had his hands falling away as he whimpered and nodded slowly. "Sh-she gave me an order," he recited in a daze.

Felicia's hands returned to his belt then, finishing with the pesky buckle in the next instant.

Both loosed a heavy sigh as the leather whispered free of the clasp.

"She did," Felicia agreed with a nod as her fingers undid the button of Zaiden's pants. "She ordered you to keep me safe..." she clarified, "... and you did." Then, tugging the zipper and groaning at the metallic purr emanating from the soldier-demon's crotch, she said, "But she also said you were allowed to give in to me—to *this*— once you got me somewhere safe, and..." she paused in shimmying his pants down to look around the room before shooting him a coy look and finishing: "I'd say we're somewhere safe now."

The purr that responded this time came from Zaiden's throat. She saw his neck stretch and his jaw tighten as his pantleg pulled at his injured calf. The pain was there, but it came in second place to something else. The purr, she knew, had been a growl that the winner had claimed and transformed.

Zaiden was hurting, but desire was beating it.

"Did you and her really...?" he began, and the tent of his crotch throbbed that much harder as the question tapered off.

Felicia watched his cock dance beneath the thin

barrier of his boxers and grinned at the truths it told. "You mean me and Norya?" she asked, her voice a knowing coo as she wrapped her hand around it. The gasp she earned was the chorus that had his cock dancing that much faster. She gave it a light squeeze, hummed contemplatively, and offered a single nod as she aimed her hooded gaze back up into his own. "Yeah, baby," she admitted, cumming a little at her own memory of Norya *literally* sweeping her off her feet in the showers, "me and Norya fucked." She gave Zaiden's cock a gentle tug as she let the last word ooze past her lips...

... and his cock let a bead of precum ooze through the fabric in return.

The sight of the soldier-demon's proffered nectar had Felicia swooning. She moaned at it, whispered, "Oh, baby, look at you," and then dipped her head towards it. The smell of sweat and balls and blood intermingled with the dusty damp of the cellar, and she knew that any one of those things should have had her pulling away or, at the very least, second-guessing her own impulses. She didn't pull away. She didn't second guess anything. Her tongue stretched past her lips, curled into an eager spoon, and then scooped the clear dome of sweetness from the damp fabric. She whimpered around the taste and felt her pussy clench and shiver and threaten to hurl her into yet another climax. She didn't cum—not all at once, at least—but she coasted along that ledge as she took another pass with her tongue, collecting more of that sweetness into her mouth before finally straightening. Then, mewling and giggling at the wet, sticky sound it emerged as, she tilted her head back, aiming her blind gaze at the ceiling, and let the wad creep across her tongue to the back of her mouth. She felt it linger there, but she didn't mind its reluctance. The taste lingered with it, and this was nothing short of heavenly for her—an irony that only distantly registered in the dark corners of her fuck-crazed mind. Then, coaxing it with a rumbling purr of her own, Felicia swallowed Zaiden's precum.

Somewhere between the journey back up and that moment, she'd spiraled over the ledge of that threatening orgasm. The slow-pounding impacts of this one had her panting—*Like a bitch; like a dog in heat! FUCK ME!* ***FUCK ME LIKE A DOG!***—and, eyeing the swollen mound that she'd just fed from, she saw a puddling wet spot where her drool had mingled with Zaiden's juices. Seeing it had a strange sort of jealousy sweeping through her. The breeder in her demanded to know why she wasn't melting into a similar puddle with the soldier-demon, and the rest of her could only lament that fact, as well. There was no divide now, no part of her that wanted *this* while other parts thought *that*. There was only Felicia—the breeder; the whore; *THE DOG!*—and Zaiden's throbbing, precum-oozing cock.

A cock that submitted more and more to her whenever she mentioned—

"Norya got one look at my body—at *this*:" she went on, finally releasing Zaiden long enough to shrug out of the robe, "—and she couldn't keep her hands off me." As though miming the scene she was describing, Felicia's own hands moved up to her now-freed tits and cupped them, lifting and rolling them against her palms. She gasped at the small shocks of pleasure that rocketed through her, the tingles in the pebbles her nipples had become overshadowed by a relenting desire to trade her hands with Zaiden's. Thinking about how badly she wanted him had her prying her eyes open—had her locking them on Zaiden's—and, seeing the effect she was having on him, she made a show of wetting her lips and said, "And then we couldn't keep our mouths off each other."

Zaiden moaned at that, and Felicia was met with no resistance as she took him by the wrists and pulled his hands to her chest.

"She was practically swallowing my tits whole, Zaiden," she told him through a gasp and a moan as he began to work her flesh. Then, smirking, she invited him in with, "Maybe you can still taste her mouth on them."

The soldier-demon loosed a sound that might've been, "Oh, fuck!" but the only sounds to follow this were wet and hungry and muffled.

Felicia gasped and staggered under the impact. The tingles that her palms had been earning were fast forgotten amidst the tsunami of pleasured jolts that Zaiden's working mouth earned. Though gravity was a distant concern, she felt her arms wrap around his head to steady herself, and the force of the push-pull between them had her mashing her chest into his efforts. She felt his teeth graze; felt his tongue swirl and caress. She moaned, shuddered, and pushed back against the onslaught, grabbing hold of Zaiden's long, spiraling horns. This earned a snarl that reverberated through the meat of her chest, and this time she definitely heard him mutter, "Oooh... *FUCK!*"

She echoed the words as she half-nodded, half-pitched her head back, pulling him along with her.

Then she was falling. It was a slow fall—one that was almost controlled thanks to the grip she had on the muscle-laced demon's horns—but it was a fall, nonetheless. She was very aware of going from near-vertical to outright diagonal, and the coursing, rippling waves of pleasure had her feeling in that moment like she was floating.

"Fu-fuck me," she pleaded in a hazy gasp, already undulating her soaked pelvis against the damnably empty air that existed between her and Zaiden's torso. "Fuck me like a dog!"

Zaiden, practically drowning in Felicia's tits as he lowered both of them further and further towards the floor, could only answer in wet gasps and garbled groans.

Felicia's naked back touched down on the cold stone floor, and a startled cry rattled up her craning neck. Instinct propelled her to lift away from the sensation, and she was rewarded with the soldier-demon loosing his own confused gasp as the slobber-drenched mounds he was worshipping rose up to swallow his face. A muffled gasp echoed up from the chasm, followed by a breathless whimper. Felicia dipped her chin to see how close she was to suffocating him—half terrified and half titillated at the idea of it—and she caught sight of Zaiden moving his face upward to capture a lungful of air.

She saw a smear of his blood on the side of her right

breast from the graze on his cheek, and she managed to summon enough worry for him to whisper, "Oh..."

Zaiden, following her gaze and spotting the streak of red against the otherwise pale mound, remedied the offense by snaking out his tongue and licking it clean.

Watching this—finding herself strangely turned on by the scene—Felicia felt another tremor worming its way through her belly. More and more, she was aware of just how unforgivably empty her pussy was; the walls of her cunt spasming like a parched throat begging for a drink. Again, she was on the verge of cumming, and she bucked more and more, spurred by equal doses of the cold floor at her ass and the scalding promise of cock just a few short inches above her.

Zaiden, likely feeling the grip on his horns tightening and seeing that his "cleanup" had earned Felicia's approval, stared up at her and opened his mouth.

Maybe it was the soldier-demon's intention in that moment to speak—maybe to serve up another *"Oh fuck!"* or something like it—or maybe he was still gasping for air after nearly drowning in boobs. It didn't matter. No sooner had his lips parted for whatever reason than Felicia's own lips were on them. Then she was tasting his blood and saliva and her own sweat on his tongue. She imagined that he was tasting the lingering traces of his own precum on hers, and the idea was enough to throw her over the edge and into another hard orgasm. Then he was tasting the words *"FUCK ME LIKE A DOG!"* as she scream-begged them into his mouth.

Zaiden quaked at that and moaned something back that Felicia couldn't make out.

Even unheard, his response tasted divine.

He was still fighting it, though; still fighting *her*. She could feel his reluctance. It was frail and shaky and clearly fated to break...

But that moment wasn't coming fast enough.

Not for Felicia.

Again, she grabbed him by the horns. Then, with a strength so sudden and jarring that it caught even her off guard, she yanked the soldier-demon's face away from hers, bore down with a gaze that seemed to rip the breath from his spit-slicked lips, and said, "You saved my life. You kept me safe. You followed Norya's orders to the letter. Now..." she paused to lick the extra moisture from her own mouth before going on: "... fuck me like a dog!"

A big piece of whatever was holding him back shattered then. Zaiden loosed a rattling groan. His eyes swam, drinking in the sight of Felicia's body, but always coming back up to her eyes; back up to that breath-stealing gaze.

Felicia distantly wondered what it looked like—what sort of expression she'd suddenly employed to earn such a response from someone so strong and stoic—but it was hard to keep her thoughts on such trivial concerns.

Because, responding or not, her prize was still just out of reach.

Then...

"Stand down, soldier," she growled, shaking him by his horns and earning another gasp for it. "That's an order!"

As it had for Norya, this was all it took to strip the last threads of resistance from Zaiden. Coiled and caged as he'd been, Felicia was embarrassed by her own surprise when the tensed spring he'd made of himself was finally deployed:

He'd snarled and lunged.

She'd screamed and stumbled.

The warbled blur of stirred sounds and motion was over as quickly as it had begun, leaving Felicia embarrassed. Her cheeks were burning—*Fuck! All of me is burning!*—and she couldn't remember how to breathe. The once stoic soldier-demon was upon her, teeth at her throat and clamped down. All the strength that had been holding him back a second earlier was now poised at her flesh. She felt his tongue travel across that small-yet-vital patch of her body, stalking it—*claiming it!*—like a predator taking to new territory. She wondered then if he might tighten his jaw's grip in the next instant; if the soldier-demon might just go savage now that he'd been given orders to let go. The thought of him biting her filled her with a terror that just as quickly warped in her fuck-crazed brain. He didn't bite her in the next instant, but, as that instant came and went, Felicia's terror-turned-titillation had her cumming all over again.

She screamed, neither knowing or caring if there was any traces of fear carrying along those screams. If there was, and if Zaiden was picking up on them, then it wasn't enough to get him to stop. He didn't bite her, but he didn't relinquish his hold, either. Instead, that clamped mouth began to move. The unwavering grip pulled at the tongue-paced patch of Felicia's throat, dragging her screams into a gasp. She whimpered, pulled against the hot suction, and drove herself into another fit as the sudden pinch renewed the ongoing orgasm. Certain that any movement might have Zaiden officially claiming her throat, she forced herself into stillness.

It was an exercise in control: riding out all those fresh torrents of pleasure while struggling to not move a single muscle. Then, orgasm subsiding—*but only barely*—she whimpered as she felt Zaiden moving further down. His teeth moved from the curvature of her neck to the valley of her collarbone, and, uncertain what he was planning—but *knowing* he was still agonizingly far from her pussy—she began to grind her thighs together. Her cunt was steaming, nearly unbearable, and it was starved for any sort of friction. Unsatisfying as the first few passes were, however, they were heaven compared to the iron grip that found enough of a gap between them to pry them open...

Until she realized that it was Zaiden forcing her legs open.

Suddenly she couldn't spread them fast enough. She cooed and moaned, begging through frantic exhales. Each and every sigh wanted to say, *"Fuck me like a dog!"* but none of them managed to mature beyond, "Mmph!"

"'Like a dog,' you said!" Zaiden growled into the meat of Felicia's left breast, and then his teeth were upon her again, biting and holding there as the strong hand at her thigh began to pull her onto her side.

Felicia's hip felt the sting of that chilled floor, made her yip and whimper—*"'Like a dog'"*—and then Zaiden's other hand was at her neck. Her eyes fluttered and clamped shut, basking in the total sense of servitude in that instant, and she was only distantly aware of the soldier-demon positioning himself behind her as that war-trained grip tightened. She thought, *Almost as good as a collar,* and then purred as his trigger finger caressed the underside of her chin.

Zaiden's voice was a rumble in her ear as he said, "Like a fuckin' dog in heat!" and the hand that had pried her thighs apart moved to slap her pussy.

The sound was sharp and wet.

The sting was exquisite.

Felicia screamed again, and she was filled with elation at the raw humiliation she felt upon realizing how much like a bark it sounded.

Zaiden loosed a pleasured hiss that was hot against her ear. His hold on her throat tightened until her shameful groans were coming out ragged.

Then he slapped her pussy again.

Felicia seized, her body going ramrod straight. The jolt was electric, enough to have some far-off sense of logic panicking and thinking, *Too wet!* Then, realizing how foolish that was—feeling a new wave of humiliation crash over her—she came again, this time letting herself lose control.

She was barking.

Barking around a choked orgasm while her master tightened his collar-like hold around her throat.

Zaiden's hand clapped down again and again. The slaps rang louder, but each new one resounded with more and more wetness. Felicia's legs were spasming, but the soldier-demon's hold on her kept her fixed; her body only flailed and kicked against him as the steady pour of Felicia's juices grew into a full-on eruption. Out of the corner of her fluttering vision, she saw the sputtering arc of her spray, it's intermittent volume interrupted in a matching tempo to Zaiden's furious slaps.

She heard him say, "Look at the mess you made, you naughty bitch!"

Then, with no more warning than that, the next slap at Felicia's pussy was one that filled her completely.

Zaiden was officially fucking her...

"... like a dog."

CHAPTER 5
WHEN ALL HELL BROKE LOOSE

~ten minutes earlier~

"*Varian's a dick.*"

It had been one of the last things Norya had said to the unbearably cute and fuckable breeder after they'd both had their fill of each other in the showers. Exhausted as they'd been after all the orgasms they'd given each other, there was little else to do but talk and attempt to catch their breaths. Unsurprisingly, Felicia had steered the conversation to her situation and, just as unsurprising, Norya had tried her best to reassure the breeder about their crew despite being nothing short of fuck-dumb at the time. She figured she'd done a good enough job easing any concerns regarding herself, Shik, Zaiden, and Kaishu, but when the subject inevitably shifted to the group's leader...

"Varian's a dick."

It wasn't a line Norya was proud to serve up. In fact, it downright hurt her to say it. She loved Varian, after all. And while, yes, she supposed she felt some sort of love or another for each of the others, as well, it was different with Varian. *Painfully* different. It wasn't the playful sort of love she felt for Shik, the bizarrely sibling-like love she felt for Zaiden, or the almost therapeutic love that she felt for Kaishu. No, the love she felt for Varian was wild and unrelenting, it was savage and violent, and it was persistent.

It seemed more than fitting that way, since all the ways Norya would describe her love for their leader were the same ways she would describe him.

Still...

"Varian's a dick."

And—*by Lucifer's forbidden fruit!*—was he ever!

Poor Felicia, just as fuck-dumb as Norya had been and looking a thousand-times more exhausted, had gotten herself mixed up, turned around, and *literally* upside-down in all her naked glory in front of a very cranky Varian. Sure, he was minus a horn and probably struggling through a lot more pain than he'd shown to Norya after returning from his skirmish with Asmorias, but the way he'd laid into the breeder:

"No, please. By all means just lounge about. And why stop there—why stop at just burlesque—why not lose the robe, bend over, and spread yourself for a true show? Looks to me like you've already whored it up with a few of my crew already. You sure you don't want to just make the

full rounds tonight? You know, see if you can't just utterly destroy that trash bag you call a pussy on your first night here."

After hearing her tumble down the stairs, Norya had struggled with the decision to rush to her side or let Varian play the hero. She'd *hoped* that seeing somebody so terrified and in obvious need of sympathy would have motivated their leader to...

Well, Norya didn't know what she'd been hoping for. Not really. It honestly would've been more productive to hope for winter in Hell than to see Varian warm up to a stranger.

Not when I'm the closest one to him, and he barely ever acknowledges how I feel, Norya had thought to herself as she'd winced and groaned with each new acidic barb he'd struck Felicia with.

It had almost been enough to have her stepping in on the breeder's behalf.

But then...

"I hate you!"

Felicia had bitten back with three words that cut so deep and fast that she'd cycled back and delivered them again.

And, even more astonishing than the fuck-dumb and drop-dead-tired breeder's sudden burst of hostility, was the fact that it had actually shut up Varian long enough for her to start in on him with the same sort of bitterness:

"But I hate Asmorias even more! You were right: I don't remember anything. I can't! It hurts to even try! But... BUT I HATE HIM! I KNOW THAT MUCH,

DEMON! I HATE HIM, AND IF IT HURTS HIM TO HAVE ME HERE—EVEN IF IT MEANS STAYING WITH A WRETCHED, DISGUSTING, PATHETIC MAGGOT LIKE YOU—THEN THAT'S EXACTLY WHAT I'M GOING TO DO!"

It had almost been enough to have Norya applauding from the top of the stairs, but, before she could've had the chance...

"UNTIL THE DAY I CAN DESTROY THE HELL KING, I'LL—"

And that was when all hell broke loose.

The entire building had shaken in the next instant, a tremor rolling through steel and concrete as easily as it had flesh and bone. Norya had heard Shik scream, *"YO! WHAT THE TITTY-LOVING FUCK?"* even across the sizable hallway and through the metal slab of his bedroom door. Somewhere in the several moments in-between, Kaishu was occupying the area of that vast distance just outside his own room. Then, in the instant after that, Zaiden—wearing nothing but his rifle strap—had stepped out from his own chambers. It had only been three-or-four seconds—five at the most—but the attack on their home had been heard, registered, and was already in the process of being responded to.

Unfortunately for Felicia, that was all the time their attacker needed.

Somewhere in the middle of that three-or-four—or *maybe* five—seconds, the team's recently acquired breeder had been taken. Norya wasn't sure how long it had taken, because—shortly after hearing Shik's, *"YO!*

HELLISH ASCENT

WHAT THE TITTY-LOVING FUCK?" and seeing Kaishu and Zaiden emerging from their respective rooms —she'd already been moving. She'd been naked and still wearing a fair amount of the fuck-sweat, pussy-spray, and lingering shower-water from her romp with Felicia, but that hadn't kept her from leaping the chasm of the stairs and landing in the middle of the ruination, ready to help Varian or save Felicia or perhaps simply slaughter the ingrate who'd dared to barge in. Three-or-four seconds, though—five at the most—had been enough time to bury their leader in rubble, snatch up the breeder, and let the ingrate slither off. Unabashed, not caring that any of the gawking demons outside the giant hole that had just been blasted through their building could see her, Norya had begun to dig through the biggest pile of debris. She'd gotten as far as, *"BOSS! CAN YOU HEAR—"* before Varian had spoken:

"Th-that's... **MINE!**"

Then, not even seeming to notice a very stunned, very naked Norya gawking back at him, he'd hoisted himself up from behind a pile of debris. He'd winced then, paused to eyeball his own torso, and then punched himself in the chest.

Norya, too stunned by his words and the display to know what to say or do about it, could only stare.

Then, only pausing long enough to mutter something to himself, Varian had vanished, sprinting out into the chaos and leaving Norya with a single bitter thought:

Varian's a dick.

∽

She hadn't been timing the others, but Norya suspected it was a little longer than three-or-four seconds. Hell, it was probably even more than five seconds. In either case, the guys hadn't wasted much time.

And they'd even managed to bring her something to wear.

Shik had, of course, still taken advantage of her nakedness, first giving her ass a playful slap as he and the others arrived and then reaching up to hoist her left breast in his palm as he presented her clothes in the other and said, *"Hot as it'd be, we don't want these monsters flopping around out there!"*

Zaiden had pushed him away with a, *"Not the time, asshole!"*

Kaishu, already perched on a mound of debris and scouring the city with all but one of his four eyes, had regarded her long enough to ask, *"Are you harmed?"*

Norya, flattered that he'd stayed back long enough to ask, was halfway through a single nod before he was already gone. Then, surprised and that much more flattered at the realization that he'd stuck around that long, she'd hurried to get dressed, calling a, *"Don't wait up for me! Go after them!"* to Shik and Zaiden.

Shik—offering up a, *"I'll never get tired of seeing those things!"*—was quick to take off.

Zaiden, however, had held back. He'd watched Norya for a moment, his eyes devoid of the lewd intrigue she would've otherwise expected, and then asked, *"You* are *okay, right, ma'am?"*

It had been enough to have her pausing in the middle

of pulling her shirt on. She'd stood there, tits still out in the open—even more startled to see Zaiden's eyes ignoring them and remaining locked on her own—and felt a cold flood of shame.

The way he'd been looking at her; the way he'd *always* looked at her...

It reminded her too much of the way she was always looking at Varian.

But there hadn't been time for that; hadn't been time to talk about it or even think about it.

So Norya had simply said, *"I'm fine, Zai,"* and then, remembering all the times Varian had scolded her for calling him "boss," she'd added, *"and stop calling me 'ma'am,' alright?"*

He'd looked unconvinced, and he'd looked like he'd wanted to say more, so Norya had spurred him the best way she knew how:

"Now get moving, soldier!"

And so he had.

~

CHASING the *thing* that had taken Felicia was simultaneously too fucking easy and too fucking hard.

Too fucking easy in that it was too fucking big and too fucking slimy to do anything with an iota of stealth, and too fucking hard in that it being so fucking big and so fucking slimy had every other demon in the city too fucking crazed to stay the fuck out of the way. All one had to do to track the giant demon was to take a step out into the streets, where they would instantly see a trail of mucus as wide as the street as well as block-after-block of crumpled streetlights and twisted awnings hanging like dead pieces from a desecrated body. That easy-to-follow trail, however, was congested with what looked to be just about every resident of the city, half of them meandering and gawking at the aftermath of something they'd only heard while the other half screamed and stampeded from the aftermath of something they'd actually witnessed.

No sooner had Norya stepped out from the rubble of their crew's meeting room than she found herself being both blocked by the gawkers and dragged in the opposite direction by the runners. She'd spent what she considered too long trying to be polite—issuing a few *"MOVE IT, ASSHOLE!"*s before starting in with the *"GET THE FUCK OUTTA THE WAY!"*s—but it wasn't until Zaiden unloaded a few rounds from his rifle into the sky that the other demons seemed to get the message.

Again, Norya had found herself conflicted at the sight of Zaiden. She was thankful for the assist, sure, but the fact that he hadn't been as far ahead as he could've been said plenty, as well.

Despite everything, he'd been waiting on her.

And Norya...

"Varian's a dick."

Norya didn't know what to think or feel about that. She never had, and she doubted she ever would. And yet, at the same time—*simultaneously too fucking easy and too fucking hard*—she knew all-too-well.

Least you get to fuck me whenever the mood strikes, she thought as she and Zaiden began running after their target. *Meanwhile, I'm getting cock-blocked over-and-over by Varian and his goddam oath!*

Before long, they'd begun to see the top of the giant demon cresting over the rooftops ahead. It had reminded Norya of the magmashark fins she'd seen poking up out of the lava lakes in Samael's lair, but those had been silent and majestic. The thing they were chasing...

Norya was sure there was a fitting comparison—something about a drunk, cum-covered glutton trying to tiptoe across hot coals while avoiding stacked razorblades—but before she could finish the thought she caught sight of a streak of red cutting across the rooftop nearest to the *thing*. It was an embarrassing moment before she realized that what she was seeing was their leader preparing to leap onto the—

She heard him loose a war cry of ***"MINE!"*** and then he was airborne.

Then he wasn't.

There was a loud, ***BOOM****ing* impact as Varian collided with the top of the bulbous *thing,* and then another—***CLAP!***—as he drove his fist into it.

"GO! GO!" Norya barked out, already starting off into her sprint. "WE GOTTA—"

"LOOK OUT BELOW, TITS!" Shik cried out from above. An instant later, with all the precision that their training had instilled, the orange sprite landed on her shoulders and dropped into a crouch. Then, content to "surf" on her for the time being, he called out over the growing din, "BOSS-MAN'S GONE FUCKIN' CRAZY!"

Zaiden, keeping pace beside Norya, said, "Feral."

She wasn't sure if the soldier was agreeing with the thief or correcting him, but she abandoned the thought as she watched the *thing*'s hold on Felicia slip. Cursing under her breath, she gave a single shrug of the shoulder Shik was riding on, spurring him to leap off and take to his feet behind her.

Ahead of them, a roaring Varian continued to pummel the top of the giant demon. A low, thundering whine seemed to rise from everywhere and nowhere at once, and Norya realized that this was what passed as a pained and startled whine of pain from the *thing* that had taken the breeder. A series of slime-drenched tentacles thrashed in blind desperation, one coming close to swatting Varian. Seeing this coming, however, he was quick to aim the next strike at the massive limb, connecting with enough force that sent a tremor through the rest of its body and into the street. Norya felt the ground rumble, knew that the *thing*'s grip was bound to fail it sooner or later, and began to scour the full length of it for any sign of Felicia.

"Please don't let her have been eaten already," she said with a groan.

"She's in the bottom-left of its largest set of tentacles."

It was Kaishu's voice, but by the time Norya had heard and registered the words there was already no sign of him.

No-doubt already moving to help Varian take the thing down, she thought before spotting Felicia.

She wasn't in the bottom-left of its largest set of tentacles.

Not anymore.

She was dropping!

"FUCK!"

Norya was moving again, already starting to realize that she was still too far behind to intercept the screaming breeder.

No longer struggling to maintain its hold on Felicia, the *thing* was able to aim the full bulk of its attention on Varian. This time, when it came at the blood-red demon, it did so with most of its topmost tentacles. Varian ducked the first, batted away the second, and moved to leap over the third...

Only to discover too late that the third tentacle was the one behind him; the one that knocked him from the top of the giant demon and sent him careening back towards a neighboring building...

And back towards Felicia.

The careening demon crashed into the wall, cratering the brick embedding himself in the crumbling surface. Then, scrambling and digging himself halfway free, he managed to make a mad-dash grab for the breeder. Somehow seeing this, the *thing* went after Varian with one of its smaller tentacles, knocking one of his outstretched hands away. He barked and snarled in aggravation, watched as Felicia's falling body momentarily snagged on his outstretched arm before tumbling back out of his reach, and, as she fell away from him all over again, he loosed another roar:

"MINE!"

"The fuck's wrong with him?" she heard Shik whisper from her shoulder.

Zaiden's solitary word echoed in Norya's head: *"Fer-*

al." She thought, *He's lost his mind!* but then, watching him launch himself from his perch and drive another attack into the looming demon's side—watching him fight something like *that **for*** Felicia—she started to think, *Or maybe not...*

When was the last time Norya had seen him fight like that?

Had she ever?

She was running, her feet pounding harder and faster with each step. Varian's fury was *for* the breeder, sure—there was no denying that much—but it didn't change the fact that Felicia was still falling. It also did nothing to change that, regardless of his intent, their leader's battle wasn't doing a thing to—

The monster staggered and began to fall. Norya's footing failed, but only for an instant. She took a lunging sidestep to avoid a chunk of debris, ignored a startled cry from behind, and began pushing that much harder. Desperation had spurred a few of those giant tentacles to grab hold of the neighboring buildings in an effort to keep itself upright. It worked—seemed to be, at least—but its efforts were also ripping the city apart.

"SHE'S NOT GONNA—oh..." Shik began and just as quickly stopped himself as Felicia's flailing body collided with one of the thing's thrashing tentacles.

It hadn't so much caught her as it had interrupted her fall. Norya didn't think she would've understood the difference if she hadn't just seen it, but she was positive that the breeder's body coming to rest on the slime-slicked appendage had been more an act of desperation. She remembered all the times she, herself, had made a swinging grab for something she'd dropped, remembered the many failures and not-so-many successes, and, recalling the more frequent in-between, remembered all the times she'd kept a falling *something* from breaking only because she'd *accidentally* interrupted its fall. She didn't like that. She didn't want to credit Felicia's ongoing existence to little more than a happy mistake made by the monstrous demon who'd taken her in the first place, but it seemed impossible not to. Moreover, feet still pounding and drawing her nearer to all that madness, she couldn't see any good reason to worry long on the subject.

How many times have we had to credit our survival to a happy accident? she asked herself.

Before she could dwell on that disconcerting thought, however, she felt Shik's leg muscles tense against her shoulder. He said, "I don't think that'll hold her long."

"I don't think so, either," she grumbled, struggling to run that much faster. "You gotta get off. I ain't—" she began, fearing a dirty joke but finding herself startled into silence as he obliged and dropped down behind her. Unexpected as this was, she was caught off guard as she spotted a few smaller tentacles beginning to whip out in their direction. Her mouth parted to call out a warning, but Zaiden's rifle interrupted whatever she'd been about to say. Three quick reports later, and they were running past two of the severed and writhing things.

Norya aimed an appreciative nod in the soldier's direction before casting her gaze upward. What she'd considered "ahead" only a few seconds earlier was very quickly becoming "above," and the angle was making it almost impossible to track Felicia's descent. She saw a blur of red cutting back-and-forth across what probably passed as the gigantic demon's head. She could only assume that was Varian continuing his feral assault. Further below, though it was even harder to be sure, Norya *thought* she spotted Kaishu pass from one rooftop to another. It could have just as easily been an eye-floater or a shifting of the light, but there was no mistaking the sudden presence of several throwing knives scattered across the length of the tentacle that had been moving to reclaim Felicia's body.

Shuddering from both assaults, the tentacled thing missed its mark, and the breeder slid over the side of the limb that had stopped her previous fall.

"It's now or never, tits!" Shik announced...

But she was already bracing for what was coming.

Time seemed to slow, and the air went still in Norya's lungs as she stared straight up.

Beyond the flailing form of the bug-eyed redhead, she saw Kaishu emerge out of the darkness, latch onto the side of the thing's midsection, and begin a flurry of stabs. Further up, beyond the all-too-rare sight of the assassin in action, was an even rarer sight:

Varian had gone full savage!

He was snarling and roaring—though the only word cutting through was the same one he'd been screaming all that time—and pounding away at their opponent's head. Almost just as unbelievable as the sight, itself, was the fact that his comparably small hands and feet actually seemed to be having a greater effect than even Kaishu with his blades.

Like watching an insect take down one of us! she marveled.

Then, putting her arms out and praying that hers wouldn't be an accidental grab, she called out "I gotcha, doll!" and breathed a sigh of relief as she felt the small, frail body land safely in her embrace.

CHAPTER 6
IN THE TRENCHES

Zaiden had a cock like a missile.

Felicia didn't know how she'd have any way of knowing what a missile was, which had her momentarily panicking—in between thrumming waves of euphoria—about the headache she was certain would follow. No sooner had this newest demon lover entered her, burying himself to the hilt in a single thrust, than she'd had the thought—*Oh fuck! His cock's like a missile!* —and, in the next instant, she was braced for pain.

Pain, however, didn't come.

There was only the ongoing and steadily climbing pleasure.

Some distant, curious part of Felicia's brain whispered that it made sense: both the bizarre knowing *and* the strangely absent headache. After all, only a short time earlier, the word "mirror" had been an elusive mystery that made her feel as though her skull was being crushed, but, after her romp with Norya in the showers—after the she-demon's casual mention of drinking straws—Felicia had suddenly been able to put a picture to the word without so much as a twinge. Sure, she hadn't seen anybody drinking from straws in her brief time in Hell, but it seemed that having a denizen acknowledge the existence of something was just as effective at making it real in her mind.

And didn't that seem to be the underlying cause behind the headaches: the uncertainty of their existence in this place? After all—*"Do you remember a thing about yourself? Who you are?"*—hadn't Varian told her in his cruel rant that she'd been destined for Hell. *"Some do. Most don't. The ones that do..."* he'd said,*"They break too easy." "My guess, though: Asmorias didn't have you tailored for him so that you'd break after the first few centuries. I'm guessing he made you to last."*

Made to last, Felicia thought, hating the way her pussy seemed to tighten its grip around Zaiden's missile-like cock at just the thought of Varian.

Made for Hell...

She'd been somehow *tailored* by King Asmorias—tailored *for* King Asmorias—and, as such, it appeared there were safeguards in her mind to keep her from even trying to think about any sort of life that she'd had before arriving here.

"Here."

Hell: *the* place that, as far as Felicia's thoughts were concerned, was the *only* place that had ever existed. But she'd obviously had a life prior to her arrival—*Even if that life was just some sort of waiting period to prepare me for this*—and, though it seemed like a cruel joke now, she *had* arrived with fractured memories from that prior life.

But why should she have any notion of what a missile was?

And why should it seem obvious enough to *not* give her a headache when she thought of Zaiden's cock as—

The horny part of Felicia's mind—the same part that was tired of thinking when there was fucking to be done—erupted into giddy cackles then as she thought, *Because the one fucking me with this utterly amazing missile is a* soldier!

And that, making a horrible sort of sense, was enough to satisfy the curiosity enough to bring her back to the moment.

Or maybe it was Zaiden tightening his grip around her throat at that exact moment and groaning, "So good!" that brought her back.

In either case, Felicia groaned out a raspy, "Mm-hmmph!" in response and pumped her pussy back against the soldier-demon's throbbing missile. She felt the rhythmic grazing of his balls against her slap-swollen clit; felt the hefty weight of them with each impact. She imagined the payload those balls had in store for her, and that was enough to have her needing it.

"So fucking good!" Zaiden said again, growling the words into her ear. Felicia moaned and whimpered, nodding her agreement. Sweat-drenched and drooling on herself, the motion was enough to have her slipping partway free of the grip at her throat—*The dog's slipping her leash!*—and impulse steered her, her face swinging around and bringing her lips against his in time to inhale the word, "Close!"

The word and everything it meant struck Felicia at

the same moment Zaiden's cock collided with the deepest parts of her, and she barely had enough time to snarl out, "FLOOD MY CUNT, BABY!" before she was howling around her own orgasm.

It seemed right in that moment to think of Zaiden's cock like a missile.

His cumshot was like an explosion.

∽

Felicia was tired.

And, really, why wouldn't she be? Save for her brief lapse into unconsciousness after she'd been rescued from King Asmorias's castle, she hadn't slept at all since arriving in Hell. She wasn't sure what sort of stretch this represented, though. Had she been in Hell long? It certainly *felt* as though years had passed since she'd first woken up in the Hell king's chambers, but she supposed it could just be a matter of perspective. Looking at it one way, she was begrudged to accept that it had been nighttime when she'd been rescued and, indeed, it was still nighttime even now. And while it was easy for her to imagine this as maybe a different night, it was damn-near impossible to believe it. For the *now*-night to not be the same as the *then*-night, she'd have had to have slept *at least* an entire day.

And she was too damned tired to believe that she'd slept that long.

No...

No, Felicia had to accept that she hadn't been in Hell for longer than a single night—that, for all intents and purposes, she *hadn't* been awake for that long. Despite this, though, *"not that long"* didn't exactly translate to any sort of shame when weighed against how tired she'd felt. In fact, if she projected the events start-to-finish since she'd first awakened in Hell, she saw that any argument declaring her time there as "brief" exponentially pardoned all of her exhaustion.

She'd woken up—naked, shackled in living chains, and stripped of any sense of self—in a literal *and* figurative Hell.

She'd come face-to-cock with a towering devil, one with a venomous, serpent-laced mane and plans for her that surpassed simple torture.

She'd faced chaos and felt the air soured by battle between creatures that dwarfed her in every way possible, and then she'd ushered off into that night-bathed Hell.

She'd been drowned and scorched by such wonderful terror and such horrible arousal that she felt genuine shock that the atoms of her body still dared to hold her together.

Then there was the not insubstantial moment when, in the middle of that gut-wrenching argument with Varian, she'd been abducted by a demon the size of a small building!

And—*oh yeah!*—she'd gotten fucked.

A lot!

Felicia still didn't have a clue what sort of person she was in whatever sort of world she'd lived in before arriving in Hell, but she had to believe that having three

HELLISH ASCENT

different lovers in a single night was something that even her prior self would have considered a lot.

Looking back on all of *that,* she figured that anybody that wanted to point out how little time had passed would also be giving her all the more reason to be so drop-dead tired. To her, all of *that* seemed like enough to constitute an exhausting week, but to cram it all into a single night...

Then again, she thought around a yawn, *I don't even know how long a night lasts here.*

And she didn't. Despite everything that had happened, Felicia still knew very little. The only thing she knew, in fact, was that she was tired—too tired to think on any of it, too tired to worry about any of it, and definitely too tired to do anything about the tsunami of demon jizz that Zaiden had shot into her pussy.

She'd climbed to that nearly unbearable realm of pleasure, riding out yet another soul-shattering orgasm, and felt that seemingly unending stream of burning-hot cum flooding her depths. Then, when it was all over, the soldier-demon had broken their kiss and released his hold on her. She didn't think it was his intention to push her away, but she was too tired to fight gravity on her own. Without his hold keeping her on her side, she'd collapsed onto her stomach. The floor, still just as hard and cold as it had been, had felt nice against her burning, heaving chest. She'd laid there, panting and heaving and relishing in the lingering scent of Zaiden. Without a care of what the words meant, the smell had her thinking of bonfires and classic cars. She had a fleeting vision of leather and metal, found it fitting for her most recent of lovers, and then let her mind wander to the sensation of all that cum as it began to ooze from her still-spasming slit. A sigh—more content than anything else—slipped past her lips, emerging as something closer to a purr, and she'd rolled herself halfway over to gauge Zaiden's response.

She was too tired to decide if the response she was chasing was to her purr-sigh or the fact that he'd just fucked her—*"like a dog!"*—but, from what she saw, he hadn't been displeased by either.

On the contrary, she'd seen that, though he'd let her go and she'd since fallen free of him and his missile-like cock, he still seemed to be in the final throes of his own orgasm. Turning to face him, she caught sight of him gripping that cock and stroking out two late-to-the-party ropes. The first had landed with a gentle *splat* on the floor between them, but—seeming to seek out the already-lost prize of her womb—the second arced across the distance and found itself clinging to the dampened patches of Felicia's pubic hair. Watching this, Zaiden had begun to say something—an apology, perhaps, but she'd been too tired to decipher the words—and, too tired to think about what she was doing, Felicia had reached down, scooped up a dollop of this most recent offering, and promptly deposited it into her mouth.

Tired as she was, she couldn't even wonder what had compelled her as she muttered almost exclusively to herself, "Mm! That's good," and then scooched closer to rest her head on the soldier-demon's chest.

And that's where she lazily found herself now.

Gods and devils, she was tired.

Too tired to think, too tired to worry, and too tired to even sleep.

She felt Zaiden's hand on her head; felt him lightly stroking it. It felt nice. She whimpered her thanks and nuzzled against him further. She thought she heard two heartbeats beneath his chest, but she was too tired to be sure. She was *definitely* too tired to care.

One for the soldier's body, she considered, *and one for the missile between his legs.*

She giggled. Then she wondered why.

What had she been thinking?

Gods and devils, I'm tired...

Zaiden's passive stroking of her hair continued as he said, "Hell of a night, huh?"

Felicia giggled again. She wanted to remark on how she couldn't believe that it had only been a single night, but all she could manage was a goofy echo of, "'Hell.'"

The hand at her head stuttered, paused, and then Zaiden chuckled, as well. The sound was pleasant, but the resumed stroking was even moreso.

Felicia heard herself make a contented sound, then she heard herself ask, "Are you in love with Norya?"

Zaiden's hand paused again. He didn't chuckle this time.

Felicia, too tired to look up and too worried about what she'd see if she did, loosed a whimper that meant to be an apology. She didn't know why she'd asked it; didn't even realize she'd been thinking about it until she had. Exhaustion wouldn't let her dig any further past her own regret at blurting out the question, and the ongoing silence and stillness was only making her regret it all the greater. She wanted to say more, to offer a real apology at the very least, but, before she could remember how to speak, Zaiden beat her to it:

"Norya and I... err," he began before trailing off into uncertainty. Another long, unnerving silence followed, and, with it, Felicia's regret began to swell all over again. "We *understand* each other," Zaiden finally clarified, and his hand made another, albeit slower pass across her hair. Then, seeming to arrive at this new truth a moment before speaking it, he added, "And she saved my life, so..."

Felicia perked up at that. It wasn't much, but it was something. She had a passing thought—*Like that first sip of coffee*—and she felt a momentary dread that she'd have another of those headaches. Then, when none came, it was replaced by a sort of rolling contentment that bordered on cautious optimism. She thought again, *The headaches leave me alone so long as I'm getting laid,* and then, out loud to Zaiden, she grumbled, "Norya... saved you?"

Perked up or not, it appeared her rampant sleepiness wasn't going anywhere.

Zaiden nodded—something Felicia more felt than saw past her half-hooded eyelids—and gave a long, contemplative sigh. "She did, yeah," he finally said. He kept his voice low as he did. Felicia wasn't sure if it was because she was so close to him or if it was because of the subject, itself. In either case, it had her that much more curious. She was about to ask him to go on when he beat her to the punch with, "I was a soldier." He paused there, seeming to end his explanation just as quickly as he'd begun it; those four tension-laced words so saturated with guilt that the obviousness of his statement was overshadowed by a bizarre feeling that he'd just confessed some great secret.

Tired as Felicia was, the soldier-demon's tone actually had her nearly gasping. Then, catching herself—reminding herself that he hadn't actually told her anything that she hadn't already known from simple observation—she felt a twist of anger at him. Though she didn't believe he was trying to deceive her, she nevertheless felt as though she'd been tricked in that instant. Before she could speak or act on those feelings, however, Zaiden went on:

"I was a *real* soldier," he clarified, "and I was good. *Real* good." He sighed and looked away, and Felicia could see that the guilt in his voice hadn't just been for effect. He looked tormented. "*Too* good."

"Zaiden...?" Felicia called up to him, wanting to reach out to him but unable to find the energy. He shook his head. It wasn't the slow sway of dismissal; it was a series of quick, jerking twists. Felicia couldn't be sure if it was to deflect her concern or to shake away some surfacing memory, but it was easy to imagine that it was both. Not liking that, she asked again: "What happened?"

Zaiden stared off at nothing, squinting as though it were something. His jaw worked around pursed lips, looking as though he was struggling to keep the eager words from getting out. Then his jaw quivered, seeming to give up the fight, and his mouth opened. He dragged in a deep inhale, shook his head, and then muttered, "General-fucking-Crionasus happened."

This time, Zaiden's tone was so rigid and icy that

Felicia felt momentarily foolish for not recognizing the name. A part of her mind tried to assert, *How can you* not *know—* but collapsed when even it couldn't recite the name. Again, he beat her to the explanation right as she was about to prompt him with the burning question:

"He's one of Asmorias's generals—probably one of bastard's oldest generals, in fact—and he's probably one of Hell's most ruthless warmongers." Zaiden sighed again and turned his head to look down at Felicia. "And I served under him." He gritted his teeth at that and gave another of those hard, angry headshakes before staring off at nothing again. "'*Real* good'—'*too* good'—I served under what most would agree was one of the worst Hell's got to offer," he explained. He wiped his face, scoffed, and then shook his head again. He lowered his voice even more to whisper, "The shit I've done..." and then let his head sway in a lazy shake. "Almost seems unfair that I was born in Hell. Feels like I cheated the system by robbing it of the chance to drag me down here."

Felicia stared back at him, dumbstruck. Hearing the soldier-demon like that was almost enough to distract her from her own exhaustion. She blinked, barely registering how heavy her eyelids felt, and finally asked again, "What happened?"

Zaiden winced and then sniffled. He made no effort to hide either—something that Felicia felt strangely certain most men would do—and seeing it made him seem all the more hardened. It also made whatever had happened seem that much more terrible. "There was a village," he began, already looking that much more tormented by the memory. "It wasn't big. Wasn't even all that special, to be honest. They didn't have anything to offer; had no capital, no supplies, and no warriors. And I don't just mean that they didn't have anybody to defend them—they *didn't*—but they also nobody worth recruiting. You see, Asmorias has always been a greedy shit, but he took it to a whole new level when he set his sights on claiming his third kingdom. Everyone serving under the king knew he was capable of ruthless and unspeakable savagery—his name isn't known throughout all the realms between Hell and Heaven for nothing, after all—but when he began vying for more and more, a lot of his subjects started to get uneasy. Any who were caught so much as glancing the other way was slaughtered, and I..." Zaiden's voice broke there and he groaned, shaking his head again as he hissed the name "General Crionasus..." under his breath. "That sick fuck *loved* the king's new breed of savagery. Hell, I'd actually watched him do it—I stood there and *watched* while the general *encouraged* Asmorias to *'push further'* and *'hit harder'* even when he was already turning entire villages to ash—and I... I didn't do anything. Not then; not to either of them, I mean. But when Asmorias started ordering the execution of anybody even *considering* betraying him—and when General Crionasus put me in charge of pulling the trigger on most of them—I didn't hesitate to obey." Zaiden made a face then as though he was about to be sick. Before the moment had passed, he was going on, practically vomiting the words: "I killed a lot of the demons I'd served alongside for years because Crionasus told me to. Dozens. *Hundreds* even. But when Asmorias gave us those new coordinates and Crionasus led us to that sad, pathetic little village..." he shook his head again, snorting angrily and hawking the wad out of his throat before spitting it across the room. "I figured we were headed there for *something*—to take over some munitions factory or draft some new soldiers maybe—but the moment that village came into view, the general said, 'raze it.'" Zaiden sighed and looked back at Felicia, either not knowing or caring that he was showing her twin trails of tears cutting down his suddenly *too-green* face. "We'd conquered plenty of territories in Asmorias's name by that point. We didn't lay our claims with the king's banner—not by that point, anyway—but it wasn't uncommon for generals to still say, '*RAISE THE FLAG!*' when we were close to taking over a new piece of land. So when I heard Crionasus say, 'raze it,' that's what I thought he'd meant." Zaiden shivered then, genuinely terrified by his own memory as he said, "The look he gave me then said it all, and I knew. I didn't just know that I'd disappointed him —that he was ordering us to destroy the village without so much as the courtesy of ordering an evacuation—but that, in my moment of confusion, he'd seen a glimmer of that same betrayal that I'd executed so many of my comrades for committing. I'd lost count of the number of times I heard a fellow soldier whisper, 'it's gone too far,' with their last breath, and Crionasus had caught me thinking it in that moment. Now, I still don't know if the general was testing me—maybe offering me a chance to redeem myself—or if he thought that maybe he was mistaken about what he'd seen in me, but, after a minute of studying me—after *seeing* the moment my eyes said, 'it's gone too far'—he..." Zaiden's eyes drifted away from

Felicia and found his rifle, staring at it as if it might suddenly grow fangs and bite him. "He shoved a hellfire cannon into my arms, pointed back in the direction of the village, and told me, 'Son, I'm either gonna be staring at a crater in two seconds or I'll be staring at one in two minutes. The only difference will be where you're standing when the trigger's pulled.'" Zaiden went on staring at his rifle for a moment longer before he nodded to it like it had just asked him a question. "I knew what he meant, and I knew that he meant it, too. I'd stayed quiet and loyal while he and King Asmorias plotted the most horrible sorts of warfare the cosmos had ever known. I'd bowed my head, shouted my, '*YES, SIR!*'s to countless kill orders, and then obeyed them without a shred of hesitation. There wasn't just blood on my hands at that point; I'd been *drenched* in it—shit, I was practically volunteering to let Asmorias and Crionasus *drown* me in it just so they wouldn't have to face a drop—and, despite all the atrocities I'd committed under their command, it didn't mean a thing when I hesitated to '*raze it.*' Then, because we both knew what he'd seen when I questioned the order—and because we both knew he meant it when he said he'd destroy that village with me in it—I didn't have it in me to take it back. All my loyalty to the king and the general hadn't been enough to buy me even glimmer of mercy, and, seeing that and knowing that I deserved worse, I told General Crionasus that he was going to have to kill me."

Felicia gasped at that. Sadness and terror and that bottomless ocean of exhaustion she was sinking in had her living in the demon soldier's story. It didn't matter that he was there in front of her, because she'd just been shown a path that *must* have ended with his demise. Feeling her own tears cutting down her face and, like him, doing nothing to hide them, she echoed herself yet again: "Zaiden... oh, god—oh no—wh-what... what happened?"

Zaiden shrugged. After all his stammering and stuttering and outright weeping, it seemed like such an abrupt shift that it was almost impossible to believe it was the same demon who'd been telling the story. Just a shrug; his face cold and stoic as he did it. Then, sucking in a dry and raspy breath, he said, "General Crionasus did what he promised: he had me marched into the center of the village, shackled me to a monument to Lucifer the sprites had erected there, and then he razed the place with his hellfire cannon. Turned it into a crater just like he wanted, and, for once, he even did the deed himself."

Felicia could barely speak. She could barely see past the tears, but she stared as best she could; batting her too-heavy eyelids in a wasted effort to bat away the hazing moisture. A few weak gasps of "H-how...?" burped past her parted lips.

Weak and breathy as they were, the question still found Zaiden's ears.

"I guess the best answer I can give is 'a miracle.'" He scoffed at that and sneered. "A very *undeserved* miracle, if you ask me." Then, taking on that cold, stoic look he had during his shrug, he said, "The hellfire missile ricocheted off one of the rooftops shortly after being fired. It wasn't much, but it did send it veering a bit from its original target."

Felicia stared a question that she couldn't even weakly gasp at.

Zaiden, perceptive as always, gave a single nod and muttered, "Yeah. Me." Then, blowing out a gust of air and shrugging, he said, "Not that it made much difference. The village chieftain lived in a decent-sized hut near the monument, and that was what the missile wound up hitting first. It was gone before I could even squint against the blast, and then everything went white and hot. I remember thinking, *Seems fitting that I'm tied to the Lightbringer,* and then—as though Crionasus had heard the thought and was somehow able to demolish that, as well—everything went black. I was positive I was dead, but I *do* remember wondering why death would hurt so much, and enough time passed for me to start wondering if maybe we were wrong about what happens to us when we die. I'd begun thinking *a lot* about all the horrors I'd committed—all the people, civilians and soldiers alike, that I'd killed—as well as all the lives I'd ruined and the lives that would be ruined by Asmorias because of the orders I'd obeyed. That was the first time I had that thought about it being too bad that I was born in Hell, and I began to wonder if I could still feel pain because it was the start of some new Hell that the worst demons created for themselves. I'd been thinking, *I wonder if I'll get my own personal devil in this new Hell to torture me,* when I felt the footsteps coming towards me."

"F-footsteps?" Felicia stammered, adding her hands

to the effort to rid her eyes of the flooding moisture. Through the blur of her vision and past the eclipsing mountains of her knuckles, she saw Zaiden raise an eyebrow at her. It seemed to say, *"Have you already forgotten what this was all about?"* but she figured this had to be the part of her brain that still had access to her short-term memory.

An even more distant, uncertain part of that same brain thought, *What is "short-term" memory?* and the whisper of a new headache chimed in behind it.

"Norya," Zaiden reminded her, interrupting all the background thoughts as he did. "She... uh, well, she'd seen the blast. It had taken her a while to get there, and it had taken even longer once she had to navigate the wreckage. She'd told me that she'd almost given up on finding any survivors, but... well, she found me: the last person who had any right surviving the attack, and the last person who had any right to be saved. She didn't know who I was, so she didn't have any reason to leave me there to die like I should've. She's said a bunch of times since then that she wouldn't have left me behind even if she'd known all of it then-and-there, but..." he groaned and shook his head.

"You don't believe that she would have still saved you?" Felicia asked.

Zaiden sighed and waved away the question. "No," he said around another groan, "I *do* believe her. I *know* she would've still saved me, and that's worse than just thinking she's being kind and lying about it. Honestly, that's the one thing that I can't stand about her—the *only* thing about her that I'd call 'weak:'—her damned compassion."

Felicia stared at him for a long moment. Somewhere in the middle of it, she began shaking her head at him. "You're lying," she finally said, shocking them both as she did.

Zaiden stared back at her, perplexed. "I am?" he asked, stupefied—sounding as though he was prepared to take Felicia at her word—and then, seeming to realize himself all over again, he demanded, "Lying about *what?*"

Felicia was still shaking her head as she answered, "Norya. I can see it in the way you talk about her; the way you talk about *this*. You don't think she's weak for her compassion. If anything, I think you credit her and her compassion for saving you from—"

Felicia was tired; had been tired practically the moment she'd first opened her eyes in Hell.

And so much had happened since then.

So many ups and downs...

So much chaos and drama...

And so much fucking!

Tired as she was, she wasn't sure where she'd been planning on going with her little speech to the soldier-demon who'd just finished fucking her—*like a dog!*—before regaling her with such a heart wrenching tale. An instant later—with the benefit of hazy hindsight—she was almost thankful for the interruption. It had almost certainly saved her from some eventual blunder that would lead to certain embarrassment.

All the same, though, somewhere in the middle of that sleepy rant—somewhere after the word "you" and in the middle of the word "from;" her mind already reeling and wondering, *Where the hell am I going with this?*—there was a roar of thunder that boomed over somebody screaming just outside the cellar door.

Felicia thought it sounded like some wild creature bellowing, ***"TIME!"***

Then her and Zaiden's private little fuck-den had a gaping hole in it, and they were beset upon...

By a living flame!

CHAPTER 7
THE HARD WAY

~Five minutes earlier~

Norya had struggled with the decision to send Felicia away with Zaiden instead of Shik. Already knowing what Felicia was—already knowing firsthand the sort of effect she'd have on whoever she wound up leaving with—it wasn't a concern of whether or not she'd wind up getting fucked. *That,* she knew for a fact, was unavoidable. With the breeder's already fuckable body serving as a homing beacon and her sweet-as-hell pussy as a magnet for anything with a pulse, there wasn't a chance that *someone* would be humping her as soon as it became an option. What Norya *could* control, however, was whether or not the demon that found itself humping her was one that Felicia, herself, wouldn't mind being humped by, and with the streets of the city already flooded by masses of crazy demons it was all-too-easy to imagine any number of *them* being the ones to claim her.

And that was something Norya couldn't allow.

She might not have been as fuck-crazed and possessive as Varian in that moment, but she sure-as-hell didn't like the idea of letting anybody who wasn't a part of their group getting their mitts on Felicia. More than that, even —and this thought *did* start to drag some of that Varian-esque savagery to the surface of her mind—was the idea of anybody *forcing* Felicia into—

Norya couldn't even finish the thought. It pissed her off too much just to think anything that neighbored *that*.

No, the decision to send Felicia with Zaiden had nothing to do with any convoluted hopes that the soldier would keep it in his pants. She didn't believe he would—didn't believe he *could*, at least—and, more to the point, she didn't want him to. She *wanted* him to fuck the breeder. It wasn't even that Shik had already had his go with Felicia or that Norya was particularly worried about Zaiden getting his rocks off. She knew full-well that he *had* gotten his rocks off only a day earlier, because she'd been the one bent over in front of him while he did it.

She *always* was.

And while Norya didn't mind that fact—the same way she didn't mind being the resident fuck-sleeve for any of the guys up to that point—it *had* begun to hurt her heart that it meant more to Zaiden when he came around with a hardon than any of the others. Sure, she fucked Shik and even Kaishu just as eagerly when they came around with the need, and they were always there to return the favor if she ever found herself in need of a good dicking, but she could always feel an additional vibration between them whenever she was being filled by the soldier. It was a chord that neither of them ever meant to strum, but it was nevertheless struck all the same.

Zaiden loved Norya.

He never said it, and she never called him on it, but they both knew it all the same. It was flattering in its own right, and, under some different set of circumstances, she might have even been in a position to return his feelings. In another life, Norya may very well have been able to love Zaiden right back; may be able to offer more to him than just any number of willing orifices to dump his jizz into at a moment's notice. Unfortunately, that wasn't the way things were. She felt a kinship to him, and she enjoyed fucking him—hell, she downright *loved* fucking him!—but she'd met Varian first.

And, in an ironic and tragic turn, she'd wound up falling for him in a way that had left her in the same place that Zaiden had found himself in.

They both loved someone they couldn't have, but at least she could offer Zaiden the physical comforts that Varian neither offered nor wanted from her. That hurt. More than a lot of the shit Norya had been through, having the man she loved repeatedly turn her away or turn her down even when she could see he was in need of release hurt her terribly. She supposed that was part of the reason why she fucked the other guys—both why she refused to refuse them as well as why she so eagerly sought the distraction—and it was *definitely* why she would never refuse to offer Zaiden her body when he asked. Though she might not have loved him in return the same way that Varian didn't love her in return, she knew that she could offer the soldier *something* where she was so constantly heartbroken by their leader offering her *nothing*.

She didn't want to hurt Zaiden the way that Varian hurt her, but she also *needed* him to learn as she'd been forced to that sometimes you had to settle for limited satisfaction from difference sources when you couldn't get complete satisfaction from the one you wanted.

In that moment, there in chaos-strewn streets and fighting a gargantuan enemy, there was no denying that Zaiden's skills and his gun were invaluable assets, but they were, first and foremost, assets that would be put to better use protecting Felicia from all those many scared, panicking, and potentially fuck-crazed demons. Beyond that, however, was the promise that sending the soldier off with the breeder presented: they *would*, without a doubt, get to fucking, and Felicia, being what she was, would without a doubt rock Zaiden to his very core. Maybe it wouldn't be enough to have him falling in love with her and out of love with Norya, but it could—*hopefully*—loosen the chokehold that Zaiden's emotions had on him the next time he swung by Norya's room with a nut to bust.

In the meantime, though—while the decision to send Felicia off with Zaiden and not Shik was a calculated move for both their sakes—it *did* leave their team minus a soldier and his gun, which meant...

"TRY TO KEEP THE STREETS CLEAR, SHIK!" she called out.

She wasn't sure where the spritely little fucker was, but she could hope that he was within earshot. With the way things were going, though, hope was something of a precious commodity. In that, however, was a lopsided and almost cruel irony:

She didn't have to hope that the gargantuan demon wouldn't win. There was no chance of that. As hopeless as things appeared for her and Shik and Kaishu, they were that much more hopeless for the tentacled behemoth.

The slimy, living mountain *was* losing. *Badly!* For that thing, it was, without question, long past the realm of hoping for anything but a quick and *mostly* painless death. For Norya, Shik, and Kaishu, however, the major concern—the ongoing need for any sort of hope—was whether or not they might find themselves swallowed up in the wreckage when that thing finally fell. The way Varian was going at it, Norya was worried they might all find themselves drowning in bits and pieces and a flood of blood and guts. Savage and feral as he was, she doubted he'd even notice they'd all been killed until long after he was satisfied that the job with the giant was finished.

And if the guilt of his past turned him into the dick we all know him as, she thought on in horror, *then what would he become if he was indirectly responsible for killing all of us?*

It wasn't a question she ever wanted to see answered.

Much as she hated the idea of them dying, she hated the idea of what it might do to their leader even more. It had her fighting that much harder, had her running that much faster, and it had her taking her own advice and getting creative.

Snatching up a vendor's cart, ignoring the owner's startled and enraged screaming, and hurrying to rip the end off of the canopy umbrella the jutted up from the top, she hurled the mass, jagged end first, into the demon's midsection. It struck, embedded in the grotesque, gelatinous mass and dangled from the length of metal. Norya eyed it for only a second, shaking off a few splinters of doubt, and then forced her already screaming muscles to leap onto the sharply angled surface.

One foot made it.

The other...

Norya barked, "FUCK!" and scrambled to grab the opposite side of the cart. Far, far below her, she could hear Shik calling to the vendor to stop worrying about his cart and get out of the street. She could also hear that same vendor ignoring the warnings as he went on cursing her out. It seemed ridiculous, but she considered the terror and uncertainty that she'd seen on the old demon's face a moment before she'd gone and made a busted projectile out of his livelihood. If anything, she'd done him a favor in giving him a distraction from the horror of what was destroying their city, but, at the same time, all that misplaced rage was keeping him from paying attention to—

"FUCK! *FUCK!* **FUCK!**" she chanted as she felt the cart beginning to slide free.

A few inches of the blood-and-slime coated metal slipped free from the wound in the demon's side. As it did, the cart's already precarious tilt became all the moreso. Norya, not sure how she was still maintaining her grip, scrambled to climb what was just as quickly beginning to drop. Between her weight and the force of her efforts, she couldn't imagine she was making any sort of progress. Every inch she managed to gain going up felt like an inch the cart lost coming back down. Finally, realizing that the cart was going to plummet from their enemy's side one way or the other—deciding that she didn't want to be on it when it did—she forfeited any effort to climb it and instead relied on its momentary hold as something to brace her legs against. She coiled, drawing her knees in until they were crushing her tits against her ribcage, and then kicked off.

The cart rattled. The hefty, unbalanced load slammed against the body it was embedded against. The twisted metal harpoon groaned and bent that much more. The gigantic demon howled and shook, quaking the entire street in the process.

Norya, momentarily airborne, saw that she wasn't going to clear the rooftop she'd been aiming for.

Not even close!

Wrapping her left arm around her face, she aimed a punch with her right at a top-floor window, already knowing that she probably wouldn't make that, either. Half of her fist connected with the glass. The other half tore out the surrounding frame and a portion of the surrounding brick.

The wall never stood a chance.

A flashback of their own building's wall exploding around the force of that invading behemoth flashed in front of her eyes as she burst through and into the building. Behind her, the cart slipped free and dropped.

A moment later, following a startled shriek and a definitive impact, the vendor's enraged screams went silent.

Norya wanted to feel bad for the guy. She even wanted to mourn him. It would have been brief and impersonal, but she figured he was owed *something*. She knew the others would all have something dismissive to say about it—Shik would likely joke that it was a shame that nobody got to his cash box, Kaishu would probably suggest that he shouldn't have been blinded by emotions, Zaiden would definitely grouse that civilian casualties were a product of all war, and Varian...

"Varian would just say that the ones that die are the ones who are too weak to survive," she finished out loud.

Norya hated that, but what she hated even more was that she *knew* Varian well enough to *know* what he'd say. More than that, though, was the fact that she couldn't argue with it; neither it nor any of the other imagined responses the other boys would have in response to *that*. She *wanted* to mourn the vendor. It wasn't his fault that all that mayhem had spilled into the street he'd been working on, and it wasn't his fault that his cart—his *livelihood*—had become a makeshift weapon in Norya's efforts to fight the thing that had literally smashed into their lives, but...

She imagined the breeder being there, seeing all of it the way humans seemed to see everything that happened in Hell: wide-eyed and overwhelmed by some savage, primordial terror. Norya imagined Felicia witnessing that moment, probably saying something all-too-human in response—*"How can you not feel bad about that?"*—and, imagining all that, Norya surprised herself by saying something else she hated:

"That's just how it is..."

Still feeling like the vendor deserved better—*because we all deserve better, don't we?*—Norya had to cut her lamenting thoughts short as she saw one of the thing's tentacles rise up to take a swipe at the building she was occupying. She didn't think the thing could see her, but it didn't seem to matter. It had obviously seen her smash through the wall on the top floor, and so its aim seemed to be to simply sweep all of that top floor from the building.

Though she couldn't see the point of impact, she could feel it. The floor shook and the walls trembled. Anything that wasn't a part of the room or secured was sent in every direction. A small hurricane of trinkets and talismans, books and knick-knacks, and a mess of furniture began to churn about, and Norya, already forced to hunch to fit in the low-ceilinged room, had to fold herself that much more to guard herself against the onslaught. It occurred to her that, sooner or later—*but more likely any second now*—the tentacle that was sweeping through every room of that top floor would reach her, and, when it did, being balled-up the way she was wouldn't do a thing to keep her from sailing out and careening back into the street. Norya wasn't sure what her odds were of surviving a fall like that, but she supposed it wouldn't matter if the impact killed her first. Already surprised that the tentacle *hadn't* reached her, she felt a part of her body tense in preparation for its final moments.

But the end didn't come.

Not of her life, at least.

Instead, it was the horrible quaking and grinding of that massive tentacle passing through each room that ended.

A whirlwind of noise arose as the world went still beneath her feet. The source of most of this was obvious: all building's torrential rumbling ceasing so abruptly had sent quite a lot of this-and-that clattering across all those many floors. Beyond that, though—rising with that initial din but rising still long after the rest had ended—was a howl of pain and rage coming from outside.

Coming from the giant *thing*.

Then, all over again, the ground shook from a great impact.

Norya rushed to the window, scoped the area below, and saw that most of the street was now blocked off by the tentacle that it had been mowing through the side of the building. The mass was still twisting and curling, flexing out of some ingrained reflex, and a few bystanders who weren't able to anticipate its random thrashes wound up buried beneath it in the seconds that followed.

Norya watched this with a choked gasp, then forced herself to look away. She scanned the massive demon's body. The oozing stump that had been the start of that now-severed limb in the streets wasn't hard to spot. It was uncomfortably close to where the window she was peering out from.

Standing atop it, looking way more comfortable on the slippery, unsteady patch than he had any business looking, was Varian.

And, clutched in his hand and looking uncharacteristically uncertain, was Kaishu.

For the first time since Norya had met him, she saw the slick-as-shit assassin looking unbalanced. *More than just "unbalanced,"* she thought, seeing his four pleading eyes staring up at their leader as he held him from a certain drop. *This is the first time I've ever seen Kaishu even close to falling!*

Worse yet, if the still-feral Varian decided in that moment to let go, Kaishu would fall, and Norya didn't need to calculate anything to know that a drop like that *would* be deadly to him. He might've been able to climb anything and hide anywhere, but part of what made Kaishu as quick and mysterious as he was was the fact that he weighed practically nothing; that there was no bulk—no padding—to slow him down or keep him from folding and bending in such impossible ways.

A drop from this height would break every bone and rupture every organ in his body.

Norya considered calling out to Varian, then decided against it. She didn't want to risk distracting him or startling him. If his wits were still about him, then he would already know what sort of danger their ally was in, but if he was too far gone—if Varian's mind was so consumed in the madness that had been driving him that he didn't care enough to hold on—then Norya worried that giving him any reason to let go would be enough to make him do just that.

She didn't say anything. She didn't even breathe.

Norya just watched and prayed.

It wasn't something that came easy to her. She

doubted there was a single demon in all of Hell that didn't struggle with even the idea of it, but it wasn't something she'd made a habit of avoiding; just something she'd made a habit of forgetting. She didn't pray to any god or any of their subordinates. She didn't even pray to Lucifer. The Morningstar had gone quiet too long ago for anybody with half a mind to see a point in praying to him. No, like all the other times that things got that hopeless—like all the other times Norya remembered that prayer was an option when there was no other option available—she aimed her wordless pleas to the whole of their reality that—*please!*—things not get as bad as they could.

In Hell, Norya knew that such a plea was about as useful as trying to piss out a wildfire, but that was what made it her last option...

And sometimes—very rarely, sure, but sometimes—the proverbial piss stream was enough to put out the metaphorical blaze.

She wasn't sure if this counted as one of those times or not. From where she was standing, it *looked* as if Varian was beginning to pull Kaishu back up. His face was still a mask of madness and rage—Norya couldn't see any evidence in that face that he even knew he was holding onto the wide-eyed assassin, let alone holding his life in his hands—but, bit-by-bit, Kaishu's body *did* seem to be rising. Granted, he *was* kicking up a storm, pedaling against mostly empty air. Every third-or-fourth pass, however, he'd make contact with the massive demon's writhing, unsteady body. Each time he did, he'd bounce off and momentarily sway in Varian's grip. On a few of these occasions, the outward swing would also offer him a few inches back up; a few inches that Varian sometimes maintained. Norya couldn't be sure how much of Kaishu's "climbing" could be credited to Varian making any sort of attempt to lift him back up, but she supposed it said something that he hadn't dropped him...

Yet!

Before a deciding effort by either of the demons could be made, though, one of the remaining tentacles made an upward swing at the two. Norya did call out this time—unsure even as she did it if she'd actually meant to or if she was screaming to her comrades out of panic— and, still in mid-yell, she braced to jump. She'd abandoned even the illusion of a plan. She knew she had none; she couldn't even bring herself to consider a plan. With Varian's name still rattling in the back of her throat, she hurled herself back through the opening she'd made. Her arms and legs pinwheeled as she cut a screaming arc across the distance. Through her periphery, she saw the swinging tentacle connect with the back of Kaishu's knees, sending a tremor up through his body.

It reached his arm, whipping to-and-fro, and ripped him from Varian's grip.

Norya wondered if she was seeing it right or if she was just *hoping* that the impact had shaken Kaishu free.

In either case, Varian seemed enraged by it. He didn't scream after Kaishu or even wait to see what would happen to him. He simply snapped his lopsided, one-horned head back towards the offending tentacle and roared.

"Feral," Norya replayed the word Zaiden had used, then thought, *He* would *know.*

Then Norya, fast-approaching the mountain-sized demon who'd taken a giant, scene-stealing shit all over her already hectic evening, loosed her own roar. Like Varian's, it was loud and savage and overflowing with rage.

As she hauled back her right fist, she thought, *Maybe I'm a little bit feral, too.*

Then Norya punched the demon in the closest thing it had to a face.

It was an impressive blow. Even Norya thought so. She could feel the impact traveling from the source and rocking it to its core. It was enough to have her thinking, *That's for Kaishu, you disgusting fuck!* and just as soon after admitting that, impressive or not, it hadn't been hard enough to be teetering the thing the way it was teetering now. Clinging to the side of a hooded offshoot that she thought might be an ear, she peered back-and-down—towards the demon's middle and, past that, towards the fast-approaching city street—and saw first Varian, hanging onto the tentacle stump he'd been standing on and striking out again and again into the soft meat there. Beyond that, though, she could see—*Oh, thank the Dark Ones for small favors!*—Kaishu, alive and well, clinging to the tentacle that had knocked him from Varian's grip. He had both his legs and one of his arms wrapped around the barrel of the limb, and, with his free hand, he was working one of his short swords back-and-forth in a repeating series of 'X'-shaped cuts into what Norya felt bold enough calling an "armpit."

Content with what she saw, she went back to delivering punch-after-punch with her own free hand, occasionally securing her grip enough to brave a kick-or-two before feeling too unsteady to continue. Though she couldn't hope to guess which one of them was doing more damage, there was no denying that the three of them were bringing the gargantuan thing down. She heard another roar from Varian, was compelled to glance back again, and, though she saw no real change in their leader's onslaught, she *did* catch a fleeting glimpse of one of Kaishu's black-clad legs as it vanished into the gaping wound he'd been working on.

She had enough time to wonder what sort of damage he'd be able to inflict while *literally* in the belly of the beast, then, noticing the rooftops and windows of the surrounding buildings passing by faster and faster, realized that their enemy—and their current perch—was in the middle of a long, hard fall. Certain that neither of them would want to be where they were when it landed, Norya barked out a warning to Varian, prayed once more that he actually had mind enough to register it, and then jumped from her spot at the *maybe*-ear.

Varian was snarling and slamming his remaining horn into the already gushing patch of spongy, slimy flesh. Norya was briefly reminded of the drillbeak bats that she'd seen working the corpses in the aftermath of the attack she'd found Zaiden in, and the thought had her hoping—*praying*—that the soldier was having an easier time keeping Felicia alive. The thought came-and-went as her nearly free-falling body arrived beside Varian. Not seeing a glimmer of realization from him, she decided to forego any effort to get his attention and simply scooped him up under one arm.

He hissed and growled something that sounded like the start of another claim of ***"MINE!"*** Then his burning gaze saw who it was that had grabbed him and a splinter of reason shone through the madness. He groaned, "Nor?" and then looked over his shoulder and asked, "Where's Kaishu?"

Norya, feeling ridiculous for it even as she said it, answered, "Inside!" and then flexed her haunches and launched them both from the collapsing mass.

An airy hiccup that might have been the start of an intended response slipped past Varian's parted lips. Norya, still embarrassed for her overly simplified answer, thought that the sound could have just as easily been a gasp. Both grunted as they struck the outer sidewall of the building that Norya had initially leapt from, then they ricocheted back and found themselves in a freefall.

Not ready to begin calculating their height or Varian's chances, Norya simply wrapped herself around him, cupping his head against her chest with her chin, and hoped—*prayed*—that she'd still be alive in the moments that followed.

~

DEATH WAS COZY.

More than anything, Norya marveled at how quiet death was.

Too bad it hurts so damn much.

She figured that thought would've eventually clued

her in to the fact that she'd survived the fall, but that realization exploded into being as an almost literal mountain collapsed beside her. The ground shook beneath her, and a sensation like a lightning bolt cutting through her body willed her eyes to snap open. She came to and saw almost total darkness, realized just as fast it was the shadow being cast by the dying demon's body looming over her, and then she rolled free as one of its tentacles started to drop down from above. The slimy mass crashed down behind her, dragging a trail of mucus across the small of her back as she narrowly avoided being crushed. That heavy, encompassing darkness returned, and she peered upward in time to spot the rest of the limb nearing her horns.

Time to see how cozy death really is, she thought, clenching her eyes shut and holding Varian that much more tightly against her.

But death didn't come.

Just the *whooshing* of something passing overhead followed by a heavy, wet SPLAT directly in front of her.

Then she heard Shik's voice call out from somewhere far off, "HOLY FUCK!"

Norya's eyes fluttered open and spotted the last twenty yards of the tentacle flopping about on the ground. At the opposite side, nearly at the other end of the block, was Shik, staring back in mirrored disbelief. Norya blinked at the sight of him, then glanced back down at the tentacle that she'd been so certain was about to crush her. There was a fresh layer of blood and slime clinging to her hair and horns, as well as across the crown of Varian's head...

As well as across the blade of a panting and heaving Kaishu, who, doubled-over a short way's away from them, was wearing more of the gunk and viscera than the rest of them combined.

Gawking, Norya swung her head in the opposite direction and spotted an exit wound in the side of the now-dead demon. It was yawning back in their direction, whispering the short-lived legend of Kaishu exploding out from those unspeakable depths and, sailing over both Norya's and Varian's heads as they waited to be crushed, hacked through the dead limb before it could have the chance.

Norya silently promised that she'd let the living shadow do anything and everything to her in exchange for such a bold, last-second save, but sex and anything related to it seemed to be the last thing on his mind. His four eyes scanned over her and then Varian, traveling back-and-forth and up-and-down again and again. He seemed certain that one of them had been hurt, certain enough that even Norya began to take inventory of her aches and pains. They were there, and there were plenty to be inventoried, but she was still breathing, still standing, and still very much aware. And Varian...

Varian was fine enough to pull himself free from Norya's hold and throw an enraged kick into the side of the severed tentacle. It answered with a fresh gush of putrid blood, a few more spasmodic jolts, and then stillness. He stood, hunched and panting—his jaw jutted and locked in a silent snarl of disgust—and glared down at it before craning his head back to scan the rest of the corpse.

"The breeder..."

Norya thought that it was meant to be a whisper, but his jagged breathing and roar-torn throat dragged it out in a growl that both she and Kaishu heard just fine. Her eyes shifted in the assassin's direction, studying his reaction. He stared back, seeming to do the same. Both seemed reluctant to say or do anything, but, since Kaishu had already gone and done the impossible by saving them at the last possible moment, Norya decided it was only right to relieve him of this discomfort.

"She's not here, boss," she told Varian, reaching out to put a hand on his shoulder.

He yanked away from it, hissing at the effort as though he'd just evaded an attack. Then, narrowing his eyes at her, he snarled, **"WHAT? THEN *WHERE?*"**

Norya blinked at the savagery and gave a slow shake of her head as she croaked back, "W-with Zaiden..."

She didn't want to believe that Varian could ever be reduced to *this*, but...

But this is *the effect that a breeder has...* she realized with a sudden gasp.

... on an **Alpha** *demon!*

~

Norya hadn't been surprised that Kaishu had been slow to act. He *had* just hacked and slashed his way first *into,* then *through,* and finally—*with explosive force, no less*—back *out of* the towering demon's body. Truly, the fact that he'd still been standing after all *that* was a small miracle in-and-of itself. But Norya's lack of surprise at

Kaishu's reluctance to act had little to do with what he'd just been through. She, too, had just been through a lot—*Maybe not "LITERALLY through" the same,* she'd been thinking, *but I'll definitely be feeling the leftovers from this night for the next few nights to come*—but her own hesitation hadn't been a result of the aches, pains, or fatigue from their battle...

It had been the utter horror of seeing Varian like *that;* of *feeling* the almost magnetic pull to submit to him in that instant.

This was a surreal and discomforting effect. Varian was their leader—*had been* their leader for some time—and, as such, they were already loyal to his commands. That loyalty, however, was something they proudly and willingly offered. What Norya and Kaishu had felt in that instant—watching a feral Varian snarl, **"WHAT? THEN *WHERE?*"** in response to finding out Felicia wasn't with them—hadn't been the drive to be loyal to their leader.

It had been the instinct to submit to a predator.

Even Norya, nearly twice Varian's size and weight and easily ten-times stronger than him on her weakest days, had felt her knees buckle with the urge to kneel.

It occurred to her then that it had been out of sheer ignorance that she hadn't noticed it sooner. The fact that Varian had survived all the hardships that he had—*Fuck! The fact that he'd survived just the arenas!*—was proof enough that he'd always been unnaturally strong. But to survive the neglect, the abuse, the trials, and then...

Sweet Darkness, and then the mutilations and... and everything else that came after!

To survive so much for so long, then to escape it with any sort of mind still intact, let alone a mind keen enough to begin doing what he'd begun doing.

Norya should have been able to guess what he was after finding out all of *that,* but she'd chosen ignorance over considering the greater possibility. Even as the evidence stacked with him gathering the rest of their crew, always managing to win them over and fit them perfectly into place; always knowing how to manage them and how to lead them.

An Alpha demon!
Of-fucking-course!

If the savagery they'd seen from him in first stalking and then attacking the behemoth that had taken Felicia wasn't evidence enough, then the effect Felicia was having on him and, in turn, the effect he was having on his crew was—

"Whoa, big red! Wound a little tight, ain't'cha?"

Shik…

Glorious, beautiful, *STUPID* Shik.

He'd found out the hard way…

Norya hadn't been sure if it was because he was further away from Varian when their leader had snarled his demand or if he was just too damned stubborn to feel the almost literal waves of dominance radiating off of him, but the spritely orange demon had all-but skipped across that distance and sung—actually *sung!*—the words to their leader before planting a few jubilant pats to his back.

There'd been a blur of red and orange.

Norya had heard two gasps—one from Kaishu and

the other from herself—and a yelp of startled pain from Shik.

Then Varian had him on his knees and squirming in discomfort that was clearly bordering on pain. The sneering Alpha had a pink-knuckle grip on the spritely thief's horn and his head yanked back to force him to look back up at him with wide, bewildered eyes. Varian's own eyes were scorching as they seemed to read Shik's very soul in the moment that followed.

He'd hissed, "Don't think for one second that I don't know you sullied her first, *welp!*" and then, tossing Shik aside, he'd steered that burning glare back in Norya's direction, finished it with, "*Both* of you!"

Norya, still reeling from not having figured it out sooner, spared a moment to watch Shik pull himself up on quaky legs before she dared to look back at Varian. She thought, *Lucifer help me! Just making eye contact feels impossible!* and then fought to speak.

She got as far as, "B-boss! You... you don't—" before Varian was gone again...

Sprinting in the direction Zaiden had taken Felicia with another declaration of, ***"MINE!"***

CHAPTER 8
BROKEN AND JAGGED

"Honestly, that's the one thing that I can't stand about her—the *only* thing about her that I'd call 'weak:'—her damned compassion."

"You're lying."

"I am? Lying about *what?*"

"Norya. I can see it in the way you talk about her; the way you talk about *this*. You don't think she's weak for her compassion. If anything, I think you credit her and her compassion for saving you from—"

Felicia didn't get to finish, and a big part of her was thankful for that fact. She'd started off strong—had known that she had a point and was doing her damnedest to articulate it—but her mush-mind was quickly losing the trail her thoughts had paved. Worse yet: Zaiden seemed to be hanging on her every word; actually seemed to be interested in what she had to say on the subject of Norya. So she kept on talking—kept on *trying*—and kept on finding herself deeper in a pit of nonsense.

She was just so damned tired, and getting fucked into a near-delirium sure-as-hell wasn't helping.

Then she heard a fresh roar of mayhem from outside the cellar door, heard a bellow from some unholy beast that she couldn't quite make out—*Was it saying,* **"TIME"**?—and then she heard something that made her think that the whole building had just exploded. She thought, *Is this how demons normally enter buildings in Hell?* and then her and Zaiden were beset upon by a living flame!

And, impossible as it seemed in the literal heat of the moment, Felicia found herself cumming at the sight of him:

Varian!

It was as though the very air he brought in with him was working her body in all the right ways. He was there, and suddenly she couldn't stop moaning and squirming. She felt her pussy clench around all that accursed nothingness—felt a wet, slow trickle of some of Zaiden's leftover cum sloshing within her as her cunt walls pushed it nearer and nearer to her exposed entrance—and she mewled in twisted delight at the idea of Varian seeing her like that.

Why? she struggled to think around the crashing waves of pleasure. *What is he doing to me?*

She spasmed at another impact and felt her spine arc as her legs pushed her ass up off the dusty cellar floor. A warbled cry of pain and alarm slipped out between the moans. A cramp was ripening in her side. Despite this, her hips went right on swinging, her thighs opening and snapping shut like hungry jaws; her legs pump-pump-

pumping over and over. Tired and delirious and cramping, Felicia couldn't stop herself from humping at nothing; couldn't stop herself from cumming.

~

~Ten seconds earlier~

VARIAN'S HEAD-START hadn't been substantial—five, maybe ten seconds at the most—but he'd been hauling ass while Norya and the others were still collecting themselves. With their feral leader getting farther and farther away, however, collecting themselves proved to be easier than they would've thought a few seconds prior.

Unsurprisingly, it had been Kaishu who broke free of the haze first. He'd grabbed first Norya's wrist and then, still working to drag her those first few clumsy steps, took Shik's in his other hand. He gave a startlingly sharp yank on both, issued a call of *"Come on!"* and that was that.

"The fuck... is wrong... with him?" Shik had demanded in-between his lingering gasps.

Norya, once more pumping her already aching legs and already beginning to pass Kaishu, called back, *"'Feral,' remember?"*

She hadn't wanted to say the other part. Impossible as it was to believe that it was still any sort of mystery, some part of her was too terrified to say the other word. "Alpha," obvious as it now was, felt too heavy—too *real*—to speak aloud. Letting that recycled word—*"Feral"*—

serve the purpose and hoping that she wasn't the only one who'd realized what was going on, Norya had left it at that and sucked in a long, hard whiff through her nostrils.

Varian's trail might as well have been a fiery path.

She'd been able to catch both Felicia's and Zaiden's scents, as well. It would have been easy enough to track them instead, but, knowing that Varian was already tracking them, she didn't see the point. Especially when the scalding reek of Varian's pheromones were damn-near impossible for Norya to ignore.

Gonna be hard to fight the urge to fuck him when we finally catch up, she'd thought, struggling to ignore the puddle of arousal at her own crotch. Then: *Shit! Wonder what that's going to do to the breeder...*

She'd caught a glimpse of Varian cutting across the street and down a nearby intersection, moving so fast that he skidded and fumbled as his tracking steered him towards an alley. The folly brought him onto all fours, but he didn't linger to regain himself. Some ancient instinct carried him in an explosive scuttle across the distance.

Norya, cutting a diagonal and gaining as she did, flinched as she heard him scream, **"MINE!"** as he closed in on a cellar door at the side of the building.

Knowing as well as him that he'd found where Zaiden was hiding Felicia and not wanting to see what a very feral Alpha Varian would do when he found another demon fucking a breeder he'd decided to claim, Norya had attempted to tackle and subdue him then and there.

But—*Fuck me! He's fast!*—Varian had ducked and evaded the attempt.

Norya missed her mark, overshot, and crashed into-and-then-through the cellar door.

A fleeting image of the behemoth demon that had taken Felicia smashing through the wall to claim its mark came-and-went as she collapsed in a dank cloud of dust.

Then Varian was leaping through the opening she'd just made. He'd landed just behind where she lay sprawled, took a blind step through the haze, and stepped directly on the right cheek of Norya's ass.

The contact was enough to have her cumming.

∽

~*NOW*~

Norya bit her lip against the wave, fought to suppress her body's reaction to the contact with a feral Alpha, and spotted a very naked, very obviously freshly fucked Felicia.

Her head was craned to stare in euphoric bewilderment at the rest of her body as though she'd lost all control of it. Norya knew in that instant that she had. The breeder's shoulders and tip-toes were planted on the floor, but the rest of her seemed magnetically drawn upwards. In that moment, she looked like a spearhead—her leaking pussy serving as some magnetized tip that swung back-and-forth in an effort to aim itself at Varian.

Despite the lewd display, Norya could see that it was hurting her, and that was enough to pull her—*mostly*—out of the orgasmic trance.

She pushed herself to cum-wobbly legs, still panting on the small, rippling bursts that tore through her, and started towards Varian.

Beyond him, Zaiden as coughing and struggling to make sense of the sudden chaos. He called out, "Boss? Is that you?" and then flinched as Varian roared in his direction. Though the soldier-demon's gun was resting nearby, Norya marveled at the fact that no part of him made a move for it.

Please don't let that loyalty be what gets him killed! she found herself praying yet again.

From behind: "OH SHIT!" And then, "Damn, that's hot!"

Further behind that and so quiet that only somebody who'd know it for what it was: an unamused sigh...

And then the ghostly whisper of an inhale that always came right before—

"Don't do it," Kaishu warned.

Somehow he'd gotten ahead of Norya. Ahead, and far enough to the left to have immediate access to Felicia if he needed it.

Always three steps ahead, Norya thought.

Varian snarled, swinging his head in Kaishu's direction and hissing, "Stand down!"

It was such an otherwise Varian-thing to say that everyone in the room—save for the air-fucking, still-cumming breeder—froze at the order.

Except that it *wasn't* an order. They were barely

words. Norya had heard better mimicry from the swamp gechoes that copied everything they heard to lure in prey. No, Varian's *"Stand down!"* was little more than a disguised snarl wearing a mask of words. It was something carnal and bestial; a territorial warning to the rest of the pack. It was a reminder:

Alpha gets first call!

And, as far as Varian was concerned, Zaiden had broken that cardinal rule.

The evidence was there for all of them to see: Zaiden's cum leaking out of Felicia's splayed opening.

A fat glob of the soldier-demon's seed rolled from her gaping depths, glided over the puckering mouth of her asshole, clung there for a moment, and then dropped to the floor with her next desperate thrust.

Norya heard the gentle *splat* as though it was the crowing of a battle horn at the arena.

Varian must have heard it as the same, as well, because he was lunging for Zaiden the moment it landed.

He roared, ***"SHE'S MINE!"***

Shik screamed, "THE FUCK ARE YOU DOING?"

Kaishu moved to retrieve one of his throwing knives.

Norya, pushing through yet another orgasm as she closed the distance, called out, "DON'T DO IT!" and "STAND DOWN!"—feeling like one of those gechoes as she did—and brought her fist down like a hammer over the top of their leader's head.

There was a loud, unforgiving ***SNAP,*** and Varian's body dropped to the floor in a twisted heap.

The static buzz that had been rippling the air

vanished, and Felicia's rigidly twisted body collapsed with one last breathy moan worming past her lips.

Behind her, Shik whispered, "Shit..."

To her left, she heard Kaishu let out his breath and the gentle *click* of his weapon returning to its sheath.

Ahead, she saw Zaiden staring back at her. He was blushing and winded. If the evidence hadn't been oozing out from between Felicia's legs for all to see, it would have still been obvious that he'd just gotten laid. Norya spotted a few whisps of what she could only guess were guilt on his features, and she caught herself wondering if they were in response to what had just happened with Varian...

Or if he was regretting her seeing that he'd been with the breeder.

Wanting to reassure him of both, she only gave him a slow, approving nod.

"Fucking hell," Shik muttered, stepping around to stare down at their leader's sprawled body. As he did, his foot knocked the length of horn that had snapped off when Norya had hit him, and he repeated himself—"Fucking hell!"—before looking up at her and asking, "Is he going to be okay?"

"He'll be fine," Norya said with a sigh before bending over to hoist Varian's body off the dusty cellar floor. "It'll grow back."

"Least now his horns look even," Shik offered, studying their leader in that moment of calm.

"They're broken and jagged!" Zaiden shot, and Norya couldn't help but hear the edge of guilt in his voice.

"Then they match their owner," Norya offered, retrieving the broken horn as an afterthought. Then, taking a moment to shoot a warning look at each member of their crew, she reminded them, "But we're all broken and jagged in our own ways, aren't we?" Her oscillating gaze had her staring at Zaiden as she asked the question. Though it hadn't been intentional, something in that felt personal. Much as she hated to admit it, it felt right.

She didn't see the others offer any sort of agreement, but she watched as realization lit up behind the soldier-demon's eyes. He nodded, retrieved his gun, then, after shrugging into the rifle's strap and slinging it against his back, he scooped up Felicia's body.

"Can I carry her?" Shik asked, sounding too much like an excited child.

Both Norya and Zaiden answered, "No!"

CHAPTER 9
WHEN FELICIA GOES SOUTH,
DEXTER GOES DOWN.

"**W**hen will you stop obsessing over your sister's business?"

Karen's words to Dexter hadn't stopped cycling through his head since she'd said them —*Again!*—at the breakfast table. She'd made him feel demeaned. She'd made him feel humiliated. She'd made him feel the same as every trashy, piece-of-shit skank who'd dared to call him a "pervert" or a "creep."

"Pervert."

"Creep."

Just more links in a chain of offenses, right there with the likes of "ridiculous" and "inappropriate," that poor Dexter had been forced to shoulder his entire life!

That was fine, though—it was okey-dokey and A-okay as far as Dexter was concerned—because others had been making him feel that way since middle school. Before that, back when he'd used to stand real close to the prettier of his preteen classmates and "accidentally" brush his hand against their backsides, they didn't know words like "pervert" or "creep." They couldn't shame him with their words, but they'd give him looks that, when he stopped to think about it, always seemed to say those words just fine in hindsight.

Dexter wasn't a fan of hindsight, especially not in regards to stuff like that. Looking back on those elementary school days always left him feeling wrong. It was the same pang of wrongness that struck him in middle school when the girls would call him "pervert" or "creep," and it had been an outright stab of wrongness that he'd felt when that tried-and-true "accidental" backside brushing while standing real close to a high school crush in the cafeteria line had ended in her calling him "rapist." A nearby meathead had saved the day by calling back, *"Sorta hard to rape your ugly ass when you still got your pants on!"* It had gotten a fair share of laughs and ripped the attention off of Dexter and planted it squarely on the red-faced skank who'd attacked him. He remembered seeing tears in her eyes, remembered seeing her give him a momentary look that was somehow both pleading and desperate while also dripping with scorn and hate, and he remembered her running out of the lunch line.

He didn't remember seeing her ever again after that.

Dexter hadn't thought of her in a long time, but thinking back on that now...

He stopped thinking about it.

Dexter wasn't a fan of hindsight. It always left him feeling wrong.

He didn't like feeling like a "pervert" or a "creep" just because he liked pretty girls and wanted to feel close to them. He didn't like how remembering times like that made him seem like the sex criminals he saw in movies and on TV. He didn't like how remembering the stuff he'd done or the thoughts he'd had seemed to paint him as the one who was wrong.

Especially since—*"When will you stop obsessing over your sister's business?"*—he *knew* he was right about this!

Felicia *was* missing!

Something *was* wrong!

And Karen—*that soulless skank!*—definitely knew *something!*

The phone call he'd been eavesdropping on had proven it:

"No. No, she didn't come home last night, and she didn't bring any of her things with her, either. You haven't heard anything, have you? Any calls or texts? Or—OH!— did you maybe hear anything from one of her frie—"

Hearing this, Dexter had *almost* been hopeful. Nevertheless, remembering her passive and humiliating tone only moments earlier, he'd still thought, *You soulless skank!* and continued listening:

"Huh? Somebody saw her leaving... Yesterday? What time?"

At that, Dexter had *almost* come out of hiding, feeling a swell of hope that he and Karen might be able to share in a moment of excitement and relief. Before he had a chance, though—

"Oh my... they didn't see too much, did— 'Followed'? He said that: that he saw someone following *Feli—* Dammit! *Did he say* who? *Did he know anything that might— Huh? Oh... okay. Okay. So nobody thinks... I mean, do you think anybody will suspect that we—"*

Whoever Karen was been rambling at had interrupted her then, beating Dexter by all-but a second from leaping out and interrupting her and starting to make demands. He'd sworn to himself that, yes, he *would* have confronted her over it, but he still remained true to his next conviction: this was a moment for sleuthing—for *Detective Dexter*—and the time for confrontation would come later. *After I've rescued Felicia and* finally *gotten to feel her soft, wet—*

"What? R-right, right. You're right. Sorry. I just... I've been waiting a long, long *time for this—I honestly thought it'd never be over—and now that the day's here I just..."*

Celebrating?

CELEBRATING!

Had Dexter heard that part right? Could Felicia's mother—the soulless skank; the money-grubbing, gold-digging, life-ruining cunt!—actually have been *celebrating* her daughter's disappearance? That couldn't have been right! Surely she was just—

"WHOO!"

"WHOO!"? Dexter had replayed the sound to himself, feeling his stomach do flips as he had. *Like Felicia going missing is the first drop in a rollercoaster?* he'd thought, feeling all the more queasy as Karen went right on celebrating:

"It feels like some sort of dream: too good to be true, you know? No, I know, I haven't forgotten. The paperwork's long-since been finalized and notarized."

Dexter's head was still reeling from that one: *"paperwork"? What sort of paperwork? For what?*

"If you can promise me that she's... well—you know—

GONE, *then you can expect seeing payments as soon as I start getting—"*

Beyond the point of any sort of doubt, Dexter had snuck away from the door. Certainty had never felt more certain, and it felt like he was going to puke.

Felicia *was* missing.

And her mother...

She knows, Dexter groused, *and she* still *went and talked to me like I'm some kind of...*

No. No! He wouldn't even think the words; wouldn't even give them a cursory glance in his hindsight.

He refused to even risk feeling wrong about anything when he was so absolutely certain this time around that his natural instincts had not only identified a very real problem—*"Felicia's gone missing!"*—but that Karen, Felicia's own flesh-and-blood mother, already knew. Moreover, from what Dexter had just overheard, Karen wasn't just aware that her daughter *was,* in fact, missing, she seemed somehow *relieved* at that fact!

No, not just relieved.

Karen had been *celebrating* her daughter's disappearance over the phone!

And I wouldn't have thought to listen in on that urgent call of yours if I hadn't noticed that little smile you let slip at breakfast, you horrible bitch!

He chased this thought with another—*"Detective Dexter," indeed!*—and then he caught himself wondering—

No, Dexter didn't know who was on the other end of that call, but he already knew he didn't like whoever it was.

Why would he?

Still, he didn't feel like sharing the blame regarding the conspiracy of Felicia's disappearance. He liked feeling like it was all Karen's fault; liked the idea of stacking all the blame against her and her alone so that when he tracked down Felicia and told her everything they could—

Dexter gasped as Karen came around the bend and strolled right into him.

"OOMPH!" she grunted, looking up from her phone's screen and fixing him with a look that said any number of words belonging to a chain of offenses that had been growing around Dexter's neck his entire life. Of all the words that her look seemed to say, though, what Karen actually said was, "Oh. You again," followed by a chirp of contempt, a bemused hum, and then a sharp and wet popping sound from a pair of freshly painted lips as they opened to say, "Not that it's any of your business, but I just got off the phone with your sister."

With everything Dexter knew—with everything he'd just overheard—the blatancy of this lie came as such a shock that he felt as though Karen had just slapped him across the face with it. In his head, he heard himself screaming *"LIAR! LIAR! LIAR!"* in her face; he envisioned himself delivering a very real slap in response to her spoken one; and he envisioned himself confronting her with what he'd heard and demanding answers.

Instead, Dexter heard himself say, "Oh?" and then hated himself for it.

The smile that Karen showed him next had him hating himself even more.

"Mmhm," she hummed through that smile. "She said that she and the girls decided to head south on an early vacation."

Dexter wanted to scream *"LIAR! LIAR! LIAR!"* He wanted to slap her while he screamed it. Then he wanted to pin her to the wall and demand answers. *"Or else..."*

"South?" he heard himself echo dumbly. "On vacation."

"Mmhm," Karen hummed again, still smiling. "Mexico, I'd guess. That's where all the girls her age like to go, right? Tequila shots and toned men with sun-bronzed skin," she said with another of those contemptuous chirps as she made a show of looking Dexter over from top-to-bottom. Her eyes flashed with more of those chain-words, but at the forefront of these was a line Dexter had only ever imagined all those skanks thinking: *"Like you have anything to offer."* Karen's eyes finished their journey and their unspoken shot before locking onto his own and narrowing as she said, "Again: not that it's any of your business. Just figured I'd put a stop to your most recent claim and once again ask you to cut it out with this ridiculous and inappropriate fixation on your sister."

"She's not my sister!" Dexter finally snapped, glaring back into Karen's slitted gaze.

To his surprise, this outburst only made his stepmother's smile blossom into something bigger and brighter. "Oh?" she cooed, cocking her head quizzically. "She's not? Then I suppose I'm not your mother, right?"

Dexter saw this for the trap that it was and said nothing. His eyes dropped, stopped at Karen's middle, and spotted her phone still in her small, dainty, manicured hand at the exact moment the screen blacked out.

Suddenly he wanted nothing more than to know who she'd been talking to a moment earlier.

Catching him staring at her waist, Karen sucked her teeth and muttered, "Creep."

The word hit like another slap, and Dexter took a step back and steered his already blurring vision back up at her.

He couldn't make out her expression in that moment, but he heard her just fine as she said, "And if I'm not your mother, then I've got no reason to go on letting you stay in this house and making me uncomfortable with all your pervy gawking and leering. If I'm not your mother, then nobody will call me a monster for telling you that I'm sick of finding your crunchy, jizz-soaked socks in the bottom of the hamper or that I've had enough of ignoring the way you're always sneaking around the house and trying to catch me or my daughter showering or getting changed." She sucked in a deep, venomous breath and leaned in close enough for Dexter to see through his tear-filled eyes that, yes, she was still smiling that big, wide blossom of a smile. "But most of all, *Dexter*," she spat his name out the same way a girl in his high school had when she'd called him *"Dexter-the-'molexster,'"* and, though Karen hadn't said it, Dexter couldn't help but think that she still had in her own way, "if I'm *not* your mother, then it means I don't have to pretend that I don't know about all those little fantasy journals you keep under your bed!"

Dexter's eyes went wide at that. His throat dried on the resulting gasp, and his voice came out as a stuttering croak. He didn't know what he was trying to say, but he couldn't get a single syllable of it out.

Karen's already impossible smile grew, and she nodded. "Yeah, Dex," she said in an almost convincing tone of mock-sympathy. "I read them—every rapey word—about how you'd like to take my daughter. Pretty sick shit, guy; always wanting to find her tied up or unconscious after 'the bad guys'"—her hands rose only inches from Dexter's face so she could air-quote the words as she said them in a nasally whine—"had their way with her. Funny how you never added the part where you untied her or woke her up. Nope. You'd just pick up where the other guys left off in all those stories, wouldn't you?" Karen let the question hang in the air for a moment, both of them knowing it didn't need an answer, before she shrugged and chirped again. "If Felicia's not your sister, then I'm not your mother. And if I'm not your mother, then I don't want some Dahmer-wannabe nerd with a closeted incest fetish stalking through my halls and waiting for the day to come when fantasizing in notebooks isn't good enough to jerk off ov—HEY! GIVE THAT BACK, YOU REPULSIVE LITTLE SHIT!"

Dexter hadn't even realized what he was doing until he was halfway through the middle of doing it.

Karen, the soulless skank!

The heartless, conniving bitch!

He had her phone!

Somewhere in her rant, he'd glanced down at it again, started remembering the call she'd just gotten off of—*not* with Felicia—and, deciding he had to know who she'd been talking to, he'd snatched the phone out of her hand and was running with it.

Running...

Stumbling...

SPRINTING!

Down the hall. Past his bedroom door—spotting all his posters and statues; seeing all the figurines and monster models seeming to cheer him as he passed—and then around the bend and towards the stairs.

He was faster than Karen. He might not have been a jock, and it might have been years since he'd actually had any reason to run for more than five seconds in a last-ditch effort to catch the bus, but he at least knew that he was faster than the soulless, heartless bitch who *wasn't* his mother!

And why would I want her to be? he asked himself, nearly making himself laugh as he did. *Just look at what she's doing to her own daughter!*

Detective Dexter *was* on the case, and now he had all the evidence he needed right there in his hand. He just needed to run far enough away from the horrible skank—needed to get down the stairs, out the door, and maybe a block-or-two down the street—and then...

Dexter's foot missed the first step of the mahogany staircase. The upright view of the house he'd grown up in went wonky, and then he was staring down at the rows of hardwood steps.

How long had it been since he'd taken a tumble down those stairs?

He had enough time to think, *I was smaller then,* and, *the stairs were carpeted then, too.*

Then he felt his forehead strike the banister, saw a flash like a sunspot, and then he couldn't feel anything.

He lost count of the impacts and all the horrible sounds arising from them, but he was momentarily aware of staring back up the stairs when it finally stopped. A distant, airy part of him thought, *Why's Mommy crying?* before he realized that the mangled mess of his right arm was backwards.

He wondered why his right hand should look like his left before recalling a funny thought he'd had years earlier when he'd spun the head on one of his He-Man figures all the way around.

He thought...

He thought...

Dexter wasn't a fan of hindsight, but, looking back on all this, he couldn't help but wonder if things might not have worked out some other way if he'd done something differently.

Slowly, everything went cold and dark...

And then hot and bright.

CHAPTER 10
HISTORY

They kept the arenas cold.
    He'd heard the spectators—all those upper-class elite vermin—complaining about this, but it never stopped them from coming. They came. They came again and again, and each time they came he'd hear them complaining about the cold. They came, they complained, and then they buried themselves deeper into their coats and their capes and drop their fat, well-fed asses into the cushioned seats and begin their chanting:

"DEATH! DEATH! DEATH!"

That was when they—the same ones that kept the arenas cold—would open up the gates and give the spectators what they wanted...

And then the arenas would get hot.

Varian, when he was still very young, asked Saroya why they kept the arenas cold. It was long before the worst parts of his life, but measuring misery was a difficult task when a soul knew nothing else. Back then, though, Varian still had all his parts: he still had all four of his arms, still had all *four of his legs, and he still had his three eyes and his two cocks. Indeed, it was a time before times; a time when he still had all his parts and was still in Saroya's good graces.*

She'd stood over him like a mother in those days, but only in appearance. She'd seemed taller and stronger then, enough so that, even when Varian had grown and had to dip his chin to address her, she still seemed to stand over him; still seemed taller and stronger than he could ever hope to be. She never stopped feeling like a mother to him, either, which made the hatred burn all the hotter.

He'd think—just as he still thought—that no mother should do such things to her children.

Back then, though, small and young as he'd been—and having no other to look up to—Varian didn't have a choice.

He had no choice in whom he called "mother."

He had no choice in whom he could turn to for answers.

And, when all was said and done, Varian had no choice in anything at all.

Even then, small and young as he was, he'd known that much. It was, in fact, the lesson he'd ever learned. And, for everything he didn't know, he had to ask Saroya and hope that she was feeling merciful.

The second lesson Varian learned: Saroya never felt merciful.

There were many, many more lessons that he'd been taught, and while most didn't come directly from Saroya, they did come from brutes who served her. Like her, they never felt merciful. Their unmerciful ways were hardly ever as terrible or humiliating as Saroya's—not unless she'd directly ordered them to teach him a more "intimate" lesson—but they left their marks all the same.

Still, as any child with his mother—even those residing in the dankest corners of Hell—Varian had noone else to turn to, noone else to ask, and so he'd asked her about the arenas and why they were kept so cold.

She'd smiled at the question and given two of her fingers—the two sporting the longest and sharpest of her claws—a delighted little twist inside of Varian, who'd squirmed and whimpered at the effort. "They keep it cold because blood is so hot, little darling. The blood of all those pets," she'd cooed and added another finger—the claw on this one not as long or as sharp, but the added digit still stretching and hurting little Varian all the same—and the already reddish-pink glow of her skin darkened around her cheeks as her smile broadened evermore at his cries. With her smile as big as it was, she all-but sang the words as she went on: "Your blood, my little pet! Oh, baby—sweet baby—your blood is scalding, you see?" And, at that, she'd yanked her fingers free, slicing Varian's insides on the way out, and presented a trail of fresh wetness for him to see.

Varian had barely whimpered at the injury. Even then —even very small and very young—he'd grown used to the stings and aches of combat. Bleeding and bruising and breaking meant little to him, a fact that irritated most of his unmerciful trainers—when they weren't being given direct orders by Saroya to teach him a more "intimate" lesson—but the things that Saroya did to him after the training was complete...

Those were the things that had Varian squirming and whimpering and crying.

And screaming.

Oh, how Saroya loved to hear young-Varian scream.

With her fingers pulled free to show him his own blood, however—with nothing but the wet sting that her claws had left behind—he'd had no reason to squirm or whimper or cry; had no reason to scream. Instead, once more rigid and composed as he'd been trained, he stared down at his own blood, uncertain what it was that Saroya wanted him to see from it.

She'd given him a moment, waiting, then sucked in a disgusted breath. It seemed as though she'd decided that the young demon's blood that she'd gone through all the effort of collecting was suddenly the most vulgar substance she could imagine.

Varian, considering where she'd gotten the blood from in the first place, imagined that many would agree.

"I ASKED YOU A QUESTION, MONGREL!" she'd seethed while beginning to drag her blood-caked fingers across his face. "YOU SEE? IT'S HOT, YES?"

The brief time outside of his body had cooled the wad, but her efforts at smearing it against his jaw earned her a fresh wound when one of those claws sliced open his cheek.

Varian hadn't even blinked at the delivery of this newest wound. He'd just nodded and answered, "Yes, Mistress. It's hot."

At that, Saroya's onslaught had ceased and her smile had returned. Nodding, she wiped the rest of Varian's mess on the tattered rag of his shirt and given the daintiest bob of her chin. "Very good, sweet pet. Now wipe yourself and pull up your pants. That sad little button you call a cock is depressing me."

Varian hadn't known what Saroya meant by that, but he would learn.

The same way he learned why they kept the arenas cold:

Through experience.

∽

Varian learned *to like the cold.*

The whole of Hell was hot, and so the chill of the arenas before a fight offered him a chance to imagine he was anywhere else. He knew nothing of "anywhere else," of course. Varian hadn't even seen the whole of Hell, let alone the myriad dimensions and realms beyond it. Sure, he'd catch a fleeting glimpse of the forests or the cities—all of them just as hot as the other—as their caravan of murder and mayhem traveled hither and thither. Wherever there were demon elites willing to serve up a slice of their wealth in exchange for a chance to watch Saroya's pets tear others' to pieces, they were sure to wind up there eventually.

Of the many lessons that Varian had learned by that point, this was not one. No, this he'd observed for himself. Just as he had when he'd been very young and still squirming around Saroya's claws as she shoved and twisted them about in his rear, he'd noticed more than he'd been taught. And the things he'd noticed had enraged him almost as much as Saroya and her merciless torments and humiliations.

Just as he'd noticed the hypocrisy and absurdity of the elites: incessantly complaining about the cold of the arenas but nevertheless repeatedly paying to return.

Just as he'd noticed the tyrannical greed of Saroya and all those like them: relentlessly shoveling their "pets" into their transports and bounding for anywhere and everywhere just to rake in more, more, MORE!

And just as he'd noticed how much he hated his fellow "pets:" the other "arena dogs," as the elites called them. Or, when the money came from other hands, the "arena dogs" would just as quickly be "pleasure pets."

It was another of the things Varian had noticed, but it wasn't an indignance that Varian suffered as much as others. Most of the elites, he'd noticed, already had their own pleasure pets—and he'd noticed this only seconds before noticing that it meant that he'd been Saroya's pleasure pet all along—but the truly wealthy of Hell's denizens were eager to sample others. More than anything, Varian noticed, was their eagerness to shell out good money to feel as though they were somehow conquering the strongest and most violent of the arena dogs. After watching from their cushioned seats as the honed and trained fighters ripped themselves to pieces, they would point their fingers at the victors and trumpet, **"THAT ONE! BRING ME THAT ONE!"**

And then they'd fuck-fuck-fuck the demon that they'd just watched drench itself in blood in the arena whilst grunting, "Nothing but a fuck-pet now!"

That was the line that had stuck with Varian, at least.

He wasn't bought—wasn't fucked—as often as the rest of his ilk, but Saroya could be swayed to break her mantra of **"NOT THAT ONE!"** *It was almost always money that made it happen, but it was always an amount that most of the elites were either unwilling or unable to part with, especially when the second or third best fighters could be bought and fucked for only half the price. Sometimes it wasn't a matter of money, though, but, instead, one of power. The great demon general, Crionasus, for example, had offered Saroya an audience with a particularly ruthless devil king in exchange for letting him use Varian as an anniversary gift for one of his more deranged wives.*

That night, General Crionasus had ordered Varian to pleasure the ever-giggling nymph while he watched. Then, halfway through her twentieth orgasm, the general had sprung to his feet, declared that the arena dog needed to be shown its place, and then buried himself balls-deep in Varian while he'd still had both of his cocks embedded in the general's wife.

"Think you're hot shit in that arena, don't you, boy?" he'd hissed in Varian's ear. "But you're really nothing but a fuck-pet now!"

Varian had wanted to kill the general then-and-there, and he'd had the added shame of knowing that he could. He had, after all, been sought after by the general because he could. Crionasus had demanded that Saroya show him her best, and so she'd shown him Varian. Being the best arena dog meant being the best fighter—meant being the best killer*—and so there was no question about whether or not he'd be capable of following through with the desire. But being the best arena dog meant also being the most* *obedient; being the most submissive to any and all beings who weren't fellow dogs.*

Because in Hell, Varian had noticed early on, the life of a dog was little more than a life of fighting and fucking.

And, when Saroya was the one holding the leash, it often meant being on the receiving end of both at the same time.

Varian hadn't killed the general that night. He hadn't ripped his way through the ever-giggling nymph as an appetizer before unleashing his insatiable bloodlust on the general. He hadn't even uttered so much as a snarl of irritation at the general's savage assault.

He'd done what he'd been trained by Saroya to do: Varian was a good dog.

And, for it, his Mistress had gained her audience with the king and received...

Well, Varian didn't know what Saroya had gotten from the Hell king. Because it was half of the life he knew, he imagined it was sex. The elites did *seem to have a fetish for mashing their higher-than-high-class genitals against one another, after all. It was hard to imagine with Saroya, though, because Varian's lifelong experience with the she-devil in regards to sex typically involved her biting his cocks, stomping on his balls, and inventing newer and more awful ways to cram as many irregularly shaped objects as she could collect up his ass. Certain that nobody with the title of "Hell king" was in the market for cock-biting, ball-stomping, or finding out the hard way if they could fit both of Saroya's forearms in their shit-chute, Varian hadn't been sure what other form of pleasure the two could offer.*

Sometimes, though—and only sometimes—Varian liked to imagine the Hell king turning the tables on the she-devil; maybe biting her tits until they bled, stomping her cunt until it shone red and gaped, or maybe—just maybe—he'd reach his entire arm through the wretched bitch's ass until he could grab her by the tongue.

Then... Varian would think whenever he'd dared to imagine the fantasy that far, *Then he'd say to her what she always says to me when she has me moments from breaking: "Now thank me for this pleasure,* pet!"

But, from everything Varian had noticed in his many years as an "arena dog" and, on lesser occasions, a "pleasure pet," nothing of that sort had likely taken place during Saroya's visit to the Hell king in exchange for selling him to the general and his wife for a night of rape and abuse...

Dogs never got what they wanted in Hell.

∾

"YOU LOST!" Saroya screams in his face. As she does, a drop of venomous spittle lands in the center of his forehead, right in the now-gaping ocular cavity where his third eye used to be.

Varian feels it sizzle—feels the impulse to clench the eye shut only to remember that there's nothing there but a gaping chasm—and forces himself to not react. Saroya doesn't like to see or hear reactions when she's in the middle of an interrogation, and this one's already going very, very badly. At the start of it, she ordered an arm's length of her favorite spiked dildo to be shoved up his ass *by one of her more excitable trainers. He'd done so—excitedly, of course—and he's since been waiting for their mistress to give him even the slightest of nods for a chance to go to work twisting it. Varian doesn't want the excitable trainer to begin twisting Saroya's favorite spiked dildo in his asshole. Frankly, he's not thrilled to even have the damned thing in there in the first place. He can't say that it's as awful as having the eye ripped out of his forehead, but nor can he say that he's been getting violently trained his entire life to endure the feeling, either.*

He thinks that if his opponent had maybe just bitten one of his cocks or stomped on his balls or even delivered a punch with one of those spiked gauntlets up his ass instead of going after his eye, then maybe *this punishment would be an easier comparison, but—*

Saroya doesn't say anything this time to deliver her venomous spittle. She rears back, snorts up a big, thick wad of rage from her sinuses, then hawks it into Varian's eye socket.

This time, he doesn't just feel the acidic burning in the wound. He can hear it and smell it, too.

His nostrils flare at the stink.

His jaw tightens and then wavers.

His lips purse, but not in time to hold back a meek whimper.

Saroya gives a victorious-looking smirk and then shifts her focus to the trainer Varian.

The excitable bastard doesn't even wait for the nod before he gets to work twisting.

"You lost," she repeats, this time sounding almost calm. The words are lost in a wave of torment from the

arena dog's howls, and she silences these with the back of her hand. Then, lightning quick—just as she's always taught Varian—the hand is back and cupped lovingly against his face. "You—my dear, sweet pet—lost, and I don't—"

"I WON THE FIGHT!" *Varian roars.*

It is the first time anybody has ever interrupted Saroya; the first time anybody has ever raised their voice to her. Greater than that offense, however, is the fact that it is the first time one of her pets has dared to do either. It's an unthinkable act, making this moment an unimaginable one. None would have ever considered such an outburst, and so nobody has ever considered what might happen.

What happens, however—even if only for a moment—is not what anybody would have guessed if a guess was ordered from them.

The excitable trainer's grip on the dildo slips as he falls away, scuttling to put distance between himself and Varian. A second later—enough time to make it three paces away—and he's frozen and wondering why he was compelled to move at all.

Despite this, it is the scene ahead of Varian that is the most surreal:

Saroya, light-blue eyes wide and those goat-like pupils dilated to nearly perfect circles, visibly quakes. Her knees tremble, seem ready to give up their host altogether, and then go rigid. She stares down at her own hand, sees sweat rising from the pink of her palms, and quickly moves to rid herself of the beads of worry by sweeping it through the nearly metallic sheen of her silver hair. The gesture momentarily exposes the tiny buds of her horns, but in the next moment they're gone again; hidden.

Just like the rest of her visible panic.

But Varian saw it. He knows he did. He's even sure that the excitable trainer, still gasping three paces behind him, saw it. He's not sure how or why what he said should have had such an effect on the she-devil, but he's beginning to regret not going further and calling her every filthy name he's ever thought.

He thinks, If that was enough to get her so rattled, then what would have happened if I'd called her a—

Saroya's hand is back on his face. It's anything but loving.

Her thumb's in his eye socket, digging and stirring the still-burning wad of phlegm that she put there. She's hissing and seething, sending more and more burning droplets across Varian's face and body. "You *did not* win, you waste of life! YOU DID NOT WIN!"

Now both of her hands are cupping his face, both of her thumbs working into the wound with the same perverse ferocity that she used to work both her arms up Varian's ass, and she's ordering the excitable trainer to come back from whatever vacation he's taking inside the lump-of-shit he calls a head.

Varian feels the dildo start to twist again, but he finds that he's already screaming.

When did he—

"WINNERS DO NOT LEAVE THE ARENA MISSING EYES, *DOG!*" *she shrieks in his face.* "AND WINNERS DO NOT LEAVE THE ARENA MISSING ARMS!"

Varian had almost forgotten that one of his secondary arms had been ripped out from the center of his when he was struggling with the fresh hell of his recently plucked eye. The pain from that had been abundant, but the blurred sight of Saroya after the fight had been enough to dampen it. He barely felt it now. All he felt was its absence; the haunting awareness that, if he tried to reach out with that arm to do anything, he'd find himself sorely disappointed when nothing happened.

He doesn't try to reach for anything, neither with his missing arm, the sole secondary arm, or either of his primary arms. He keeps all three down and at his sides, just as he's been taught.

All the same, the three hands at the end of them are balled into fists.

"Already spoke outta turn to the mistress," *the excitable trainer grumbles from behind as he gives the dildo a sharp twist.* "An' now it's lookin' like he wanna try takin' a swing at'cha, too!"

Saroya's assault on Varian's eye socket relaxes and then relents as she takes a step back to study his fists. She looks almost wounded.

Varian is thinking "almost wounded" doesn't look wounded enough.

Still, he can't bring himself to attack her; can't even muster up the will to speak to her again.

He had *won that fight! Lost arm or no—lost eye or no—he'd still left the arena with his life, which was more than anyone could say for the other dog.*

And—OH!—how the elite's hollered and cheered when he had! With their fat, well-fed asses on their cush-

ioned seats, reveling in the rising heat from all that blood...

He'd won!

He HAD!

But in Saroya's den, her word was law, and the law was what was real.

If she said Varian lost the fight, then Varian lost the fight.

The same way he's already lost this fight against her and her excitable trainer.

Simple as that.

Saroya purrs and rolls the knuckles of her right hand down Varian's cheek. "You want to hurt me, don't you, dog?" *she asks in the same voice she always uses when asking questions that she's already answered for herself:*

"You want me to let you sleep, don't you?"

"You want something to eat, don't you?"

"You want me to fuck you, don't you?"

Varian has spent his entire life hearing her ask those questions. On a few of the occasions he'd watched her ask her other, less observant dogs those sorts of questions, he'd seen what daring to answer got them. He can't remember how he learned to not answer—whether he was too young and too damaged by the results of his own answering, or if he'd just had the slippery memory of youth but had seen another make the mistake—but he knows now just as he's always known to not say anything. This question, after all, is a much more dangerous question than all the others, and its answer is that much more dangerous.

Because, yes, Varian wants to hurt her.

Even missing an arm and minus an eye, he knows he can.

And he even has a weapon within reach!

He's not bound or confined; not restrained in any way other than the discipline he's been conditioned with. He's remained still and obedient, just as he had while letting Saroya's excitable trainer shove her favorite toy inside him while patiently awaiting his mistress's scolding.

He could put that lonely secondary arm on his back to work and have that excitable trainer by the throat. It could happen in less time than it would take him to blink. He's been trained his entire life for such a thing; trained his entire life to be violent; to be quick and precise...

To be deadly!

With his hands free and nothing to stop him, he could have that excitable trainer subdued and that spiked dildo pulled free in no time. Then it'd just be him and Saroya and her favorite toy. Then he could—

"Should have done it when you had the chance," Saroya coos...

And then the excitable trainer is ripping out Varian's other secondary arm.

He barely feels it over the shock and humiliation. What hurts most is the thought that follows:

Only two arms? Just like everyone else; everyone who's so much more than I am? So what am I now?

And, as though she can read his thoughts, Saroya cackles and screams, "NOTHING! YOU'RE NOTHING! AND THAT'S ALL YOU'LL HAVE EVER BEEN!"

Then, in a twisted moment that he can hardly believe

is real, she's on her knees and yanking his secondary cock out of its sheathe. She has to lift his primary cock and yank his ballsack taut to get to it, and she does neither of these things gently. Not that she's ever been gentle, *Varian thinks as he tries to follow his mistress's actions through tear-and-pain-blurred vision. It's a futile effort. He can't see a thing. He can only feel her long, sharp claws probing into the sheathe and pulling the smaller of his cocks out into the open.*

It hurts for more reasons than he's able to count in that instant.

Nevermind the obvious agony that the process is putting him through. Nevermind the fact that he's learned from years of conditioning to not let it emerge in his mistress's sight and that having it out has become incredibly uncomfortable as a result. And nevermind the fact that most of the elites he'd been whored out to were disgusted by the thought of it. No, what hurts most about Saroya's actions is that Varian already knows what she has in mind.

It might be his secondary cock, but it's also his breeding cock. Most of the other dogs in her den were neutered when they were young, but Varian got to keep his secondary cock because he proved himself to be the strongest early on. Saroya saw value in him then, and she'd said so.

Looking back on it, that was the nicest thing she'd ever said to him.

"Even when you're too old and broken to fight, you'll still make a magnificent stud, my sweet darling."

He thinks, Guess I'm no longer of value...

Then, as the excitable guard begins to tear one of his legs out of his hip, Saroya sucks that secondary cock into her mouth and keeps on sucking until she's forced the full length of it into the venomous sack that her mouth has become.

The acidic saliva that she'd been spitting in his face begins to work immediately.

Varian is shrieking now, loud and hard enough to drown out the sound of the guard ridding him off his other leg.

Two eyes...

Two arms...

Two legs...

And now, thanks to his mistress's hellish blowjob, only one cock.

He thinks, I could've just died in the burning-hot arena.

He thinks, She could've just killed me.

And, again, he thinks, What am I now?

Saroya bites down, but there's no resistance and no pain. There's barely anything left to bite through. She pulls back, turns her head, and spits a sizzling wad of reddening meat to the floor. Then, looking up and into his horrified gaze, she shows him that wide, motherly smile and says, "Why the long face, darling? You know I never swallow."

CHAPTER 11
"LET'S GET THAT RAGE-NUT OUT OF YOU"

Varian thought he heard a voice that wasn't Saroya's say, "Sorry for this, boss."

Then he dreamed of Saroya and her excitable guard finishing with him.

He heard the guard in his dreams grumble, *"Don't think he's comin' back from this."*

He heard Saroya's acidic laugh in his dreams; heard her answer, *"One less loser dog."*

Then he thought he felt somebody at his primary cock—his *only* cock—and heard them say, "Can you hear me, dog? Make yourself useful! Get hard!"

Varian tried to obey, but it wasn't easy. He'd been tortured and mutilated and left to die at the bottom of a ditch.

"That the best you can do? Pathetic! You're an even bigger loser than I thought if you can't even... Oh? Was that a twitch just now? Yeah! Yeah, this is how you like it, isn't it, *dog*? Like having your face wiped in the mess of your own life, don't you? DON'T YOU?"

And—Lucifer curse him again and again—Varian did. Even tortured and mutilated and left to die at the bottom of a ditch, he liked to feel valuable; liked to feel useful. Somebody was at his primary cock—*my* **ONLY** *cock now!*—and they were giving orders and making him feel valuable and useful.

Who was he—*What am I now?*—to not obey?

Still struggling to not die at the bottom of that ditch, he did what he'd been trained to do his entire life: he didn't talk back, he didn't struggle, and he obeyed.

He felt himself getting hard; felt the someone who was rubbing his cock begin to stroke its length. It felt gentle, and that was nice. He'd never felt it that way before; didn't know it could feel that way.

Tension and worry melted away, making it easier to strive for survival at the bottom of that ditch. Not having to worry about whoever was giving him orders burning him or ripping pieces off of him made it easier to obey. All that was left was the worry about how he was supposed to pull himself out of there with only half of his limbs.

He didn't even know how he was supposed to stand on only two legs, but...

The stranger stroking his cock felt nice. It was almost nice enough to forget the pain and the anger...

And the *hatred!*

By Jehovah's scalding light, did Varian ever hate the elites! And that hatred paled in comparison to the hate in his heart that he reserved for General Crionasus and King Asmorias! But even that was nothing compared to the peak of his mountain of hatred.

No, that all-defining point was reserved for the one who'd put him through all of it and then left him, tortured and mutilated and dying at the bottom of a ditch:

Saroya!

There wasn't a soul in any realm or any dimension that Varian could ever bring himself to hate as much as he hated Saroya!

"There's a good boy!" the voice praised. "There's a good dog. Stay nice and hard for me, okay? Just like that! Don't fail like you failed everything else!"

"N-no..." he groaned into the darkness, hoping the one giving the orders could hear him.

He didn't want to fail them, too; didn't want another disappointment staining his life. He had to obey! Had to...

"Be... good," he promised. "P-please, just... don't leave me like she—"

"I'm not going anywhere, dog! Not so long as you're a good boy and stay hard for me! Just relax and let me finish you off, okay?"

Their words were kind and stern. Their touch was soft and gentle.

Varian promised he'd be a good boy. He stayed hard. He relaxed.

"Good! That's good, boss! Maybe you're not as big a loser as they say, huh? Maybe there's hope for you yet. Now..."

"Boss"?

Varian didn't understand that. Not at first. He hadn't known anybody who would've called him that when he was fighting in the arenas or fucking in the chambers of the elites.

Saroya would certainly never call him "boss."

Still, the words were stern and demanding, and the tone was familiar. Varian had to obey; had to—

He heard a hungry-sounding hum and felt hot wetness envelope his cock. A moment of panic flared—he thought, *She's come back to melt off the other one!*—and then the wetness lifted long enough for that voice, strong and commanding, to say, "I told you to stay hard, dog! Or is that too much for a loser mutt like you to handle?"

Obey! Obey! Obey!

And so Varian did as he was told.

Even if it was her—even if it was Saroya coming back to do to his primary what she'd done to the secondary— then he still had to be obedient.

"D-don't want... to lose it," he whimpered.

"And you won't," the stranger promised, "so long as you do what I say and stay hard!"

Varian wasn't sure why, but he believed them. Believing them made it easier to relax again, and relaxing made it easier to stay hard.

Again, the hot wetness was upon him, around him. It didn't burn him, though; not like Saroya's venom. It was nice. It was...

"Boss"?

Varian blinked, felt a few needles of light punch through his lids and stab into his eyes, and suddenly he was out of the ditch.

"Boss"!

Then he was out of the dream.

Varian remembered the voice—remembered the only soul who insisted on calling him "boss"—and he looked down to see—

"Norya!" he growled, starting to pull himself up at the sight of the she-demon's head bobbing on his cock.

A large, strong hand caught him in the chest and pushed him back down as she raised her head and fixed him with a look he'd never seen before.

"I thought you said you'd be good, *dog!*" she hissed at him as she continued to stroke his cock with the hand that wasn't pinning him down. "Or have you become such a monumental failure since losing that fight and all those parts of yourself that you don't even know how to shut up and play dead?"

Varian wanted to throw her off of him and curse her out. He knew he could do it, too; knew Norya didn't have it in her to go against him, but...

But that look!

And her voice!

Varian *wanted* to make Norya stop, but he couldn't bring himself to act. Hard as he pushed for his muscles to move and his voice to emerge, he couldn't. He could only stare, fists clenched but dormant at his sides as they'd been before, and watch as Norya kept that dominating stare locked back on him.

She never stopped stroking him as she let the moment pass, then, as a flutter of submission floated across Varian, he felt his expression soften.

Norya saw this and gave a single nod. She asked, "You gonna be a good dog for me?" but her eyes seemed to say something else.

In the back parts of Varian's thoughts, where bits of that sleepiness still lingered, he thought he remembered hearing, *"Sorry for this, boss."*

And then Varian understood.

He couldn't remember much after the attack on their base—after *something* had made off with the breeder—but, in *not* remembering, he knew that it must not have been good. More had gone wrong in that instant than just a demolished wall and a stolen hostage, and his second-in-command—the only demon he really, truly trusted—was doing what she had to do.

Not that it mattered.

With her throwing around orders and demeaning him like that, some hardwired part of him wouldn't allow him to fight it.

He thought, *As clever as she is strong,* and then he nodded and said, "Y-yes, Mistress."

It burned his cheeks to say the words again after all this time, and it burnt his soul to say it to Norya, but the words were out before he'd even considered what he was about to say.

But Norya didn't shame him for it. She just said, "There's a good boy," and, "Now let's get that rage-nut out of you, huh?" and then went back to sucking his cock.

Varian didn't know what she meant by that, but he forgot it just as quickly.

The she-demon's mouth was exquisite!

He felt her tongue swim around the perimeter of his flared cockhead, then moaned as it spiraled inward to tease the slit. She repeated the motion a few times, mewled happily as Varian groaned around a fresh wave of pleasure, and then she began to sink her head lower...

And lower...

And lower.

Varian heard his panting breaths hike an octave with each new inch Norya swallowed, and, like the words that had slipped out, he was almost embarrassed to hear his own reaction to her treatment but couldn't bring himself to stop. He trembled at the onslaught and, either working to restrain him again or simply putting the hand that was still on his chest to better use, Norya reached up and took him by the throat. The pressure earned another gasp as memories of his training collar flashed in his mind, and all the *"good boy"*s he'd heard as a boy cycled back into the forefront of his thoughts.

He thought, *"I must be good."*

He thought, *"I am good."*

Then he felt his cockhead reach the back of Norya's throat, heard her groan—felt the rumble of it travel through his shaft—and then heard the hungry, gagging *"GLORB!"* as she shoved his cock past the barrier. There was a momentary tug as his cock bent to continue its journey down the stretch of her gullet, but the discomfort was immediately foreshadowed by the overwhelming euphoria of the new sensation.

Norya's throat muscles—simultaneously struggling to pull in air even as she worked to swallow more and more of him—rippled and tightened around him. Struck with a sudden disbelief that she'd managed to take so much of him and awestruck by the curiosity of it, he craned his head around the grip at his throat and watched as

Norya's throat bulged and swelled more and more as she continued to shove his full length into her mouth.

He felt a moment of impossible pride in both of them, equally stunned by Norya's abilities as well as his own size. Submissive as he'd become in that instant, it felt wrong to boast—even if only to himself—about the length of his cock, but the moment he tried to degrade himself he found himself thinking, *But just look at what it's doing to such a giant demon's throat!*

And, truly, the effect was undeniable. It might have been horrifying if it wasn't driving Varian so wild with the sheer eroticism of it. Norya's neck was stretched to a point that seemed almost unbearable to witness, but, despite this, he couldn't resist reaching out and taking her by the horns. His fingers wrapped around the coiled lengths on either side of her head, and he more felt than heard a satisfied purr as he did.

He gave a light, experimental pull.

Norya's head sank further, her lips driving into the base and mashing against his groin and balls. Ignoring the nest of hair she was all-but kissing in that instant, she worked her lips and tongue against the surface, nursing it and humming contently.

Varian felt the tip of her tongue just above his balls and distantly thought of the sheathe that rested there; the sheathe that used to contain his secondary breeder's cock. He had a wandering thought of that swirling tongue tickling the pointed head of that now-missing cock, and the fantasy was almost enough to have him feeling the tickle of it.

But, having woken from many a dream of his prior

life *certain* he could feel the viscera clinging to hands and feet he no longer possessed, he knew all-too-well the power of thoughts when it came to phantom limbs.

Still clinging to Norya's horns, he yanked upward, grossly captivated at how far he had to pull—how long it took—to bring the head of his cock back up from her gullet and to the panting ring of her lips. Gasping and groaning—sounding close to the edge, herself—the she-demon growled, "That's it, *dog!* Be a good pet and fuck my face!"

On any other night, Varian wouldn't have let it get this far. Hell, he'd managed to resist all urges and desires since the day he'd managed to drag himself out of that ditch. Certain as he was that nobody would want a mutilated dog—committed as he was to never let another bear witness to the effects of that mutilation—it wasn't hard to refuse the offers Norya had made since then.

Now, however...

Well, it was different now.

There was some new need. Something—*"Now let's get that rage-nut out of you, huh?"*—that was almost an ache that was driving him then. Then, of course, there was the raw, pent-up pleasure of it all. More than that, though, was the burning need. He had the discipline to ignore instincts and disregard baser desires, but what he couldn't bear was...

Gotta be good! Can't fail again!

He'd been given a command, and Varian had to obey.

So, clutching the she-demon by the horns and forgetting everything else, he fucked Norya's face. The hot, wet, and rhythmic *glorp-glorp-glorp*s started going

HELLISH ASCENT

faster and faster as worry for her wellbeing drifted away. With each passing second, he found himself feeling more and more foolish for ever worrying at all. Uncertain how she could be breathing through the oral assault —beginning to suspect that she wasn't breathing at all— he came to realize that Norya was no longer on the edge.

She was cumming!

Hard!

Doubt in this was short-lived, as one of the passes that once more freed her throat had a stifled cry of "—UMMING! FUCK! I'M CUMM—*GLURG!*" flooding the room.

The wanton depravity of it—the thought that this brutal warrior of a she-demon could be brought to orgasm through such a savage and relentless attack on her throat —had Varian feeling an ancient-yet-familiar pressure building that had him crying out long before his actual release. Realizing what was coming and remembering how long it had been, he once more began to worry for Norya's safety. A nightmarish thought of drowning her or flooding her lungs forced a near-sob from his otherwise ecstatic wails, and he worked to pull her head off of his throbbing cock.

"C-can't... *Won't* cum in your—" he tried to warn her.

But Norya wouldn't hear another word of it.

The wide, pulsing rim of his cockhead had all-but breached the spit-slicked opening of her mouth before she snarled, "DON'T YOU FUCKING DARE, DOG!" and slammed her head back down the rest of the way.

The full length of Varian's cock vanished back into

Norya's throat with a resounding *"UUMPH!"* and, halfway through its journey, he began to cum.

The first rocket visibly rippled the flesh of the she-demon's neck as it began to gather before being shoved down by the still-erupting source. Then her lips were back at his base, the seal closed off, and the sound of her muffled gulps echoing through his spasming rod.

When, at last, the torrent had calmed to a lazy trickle, Norya eventually started to pull her head back up. She was slow and gentle, her bright yellow eyes already looking up at him with a mixture of pride and sorrow. Then, as his deflating cockhead slipped free from her lips with a lazy *plop,* she licked away some of the excess, gave a sincere kiss to the shimmering crown, and stared up at him.

Finally, after clearing her throat, she said, "I'm sorry I said those things, boss. I just really needed you to clear your head after everything that happened."

Varian, definitely feeling more clearheaded than he had in a while, struggled to look back at her as he hurried to get dressed. Nodding, hoping it reflected the appreciation he couldn't get out in words, he asked, "So... what *did* happen?"

∽

Norya felt dirty.

This didn't come as a shock to her at that moment, but it would have shocked her if she'd been told it would be this way. She'd been enthusiastically serving as their team's resident cum-dump for some time, and she'd never felt dirty before. She'd been filthy and depraved with Shik; she'd been rough and nasty with Zaiden; and she'd been tender and passionate with Kaishu. Sometimes, when more than one of the guys was in the mood at the same time—or if Norya was feeling particularly needy and decided to call in some favors—she'd even found ways to take on more than one of them at a time. It was always fun, it always felt good, and she always came out of it satisfied...

And *not* feeling dirty.

While she *liked* the guys and *loved* to fuck them, though, it was no secret that she didn't love them. Not like Zaiden loved her, for one, but also not like how she loved Varian. Varian, however, was untouchable. Or, rather, he *had* been. It was a fact that Norya had loathed for some time, but it was an indisputable fact and one without exceptions. And, because she had known Varian as long as she had, she'd never resented that fact, either.

It was, after all, she who had found him near-death after what that heinous bitch had done to him, and it was she that he'd entrusted his secrets to while she'd nursed him back to health. She knew that she'd fallen in love with him somewhere in that time, but, after hearing about the rape and torture and whoring—not to mention the hell he'd been pushed through as an arena fighter his entire life—as well as the horrific scene of the mutilation and dismemberment that had put him in the ditch she'd found him in, Norya also knew how Varian felt. From the moment she'd met him, he'd seen himself as a broken, worthless thing; a dog that had since lost the right to even be called that much. She'd assured him then and ever since then that he passed quite well as any of the other two-armed, two-legged, and two-eyed demons, but those assurances never kept him from feeling like a deformed monster. Maybe he'd stopped saying it—having all those others around made for a lot less private time to sit around and chat like they used to—but Norya knew. It was the same way she knew as much now as she had on that first day that, though she loved him, she'd never be able to touch him. The life that had driven him into that ditch had stained him from contact, and it was obvious that the only thing that Varian hated more than what he'd been "turned into" was the idea of anybody else trying to touch it.

Not that Norya could blame him.

Not after everything that had been said and done to him.

Past-Norya would have been elated to know that she'd eventually get to get her hands on Varian; that she'd get to get her mouth on him, to get him *inside* her in *any* way. Past-her would have trumpeted with joy if she'd been told that the day would come when the demon she loved finally stopped resisting and actually went so far as to grab her and thrust with the sort of fervor he had only moments ago. And if some magic force had allowed past-her to know that she would have the taste of Varian's cum on her tongue while a massive load of the stuff was sloshing in her belly—*exactly* the way it was now—then she'd be eagerly counting down the seconds until that moment finally arrived.

But now that it had arrived, she couldn't revel in it the way she would have liked. Instead, the abysmal night they'd just gone through had forced her to do something that made her feel dirty. Varian had been wild—*feral!*—and his Alpha instincts were driving him into a frenzy that was going to get somebody hurt or possibly even killed. Miserable as Varian was because of his past, he'd have an even greater layer of it added to it if something had happened to a member of his crew. Moreover, all of his efforts—all of *their* efforts—would suddenly mean nothing if something had happened to him.

That had been the driving thought for Norya when she'd knocked him out in that basement, and it had been the driving thought behind her thoughts while she'd carried him back to what remained of their headquarters. It had stuck, driving her all the further as they worked to secure the building as best they could despite missing a portion of its front wall, and, by the time they had finished, it had driven her to carry him back to his chambers, ready to do something that she already felt dirty for having to do.

But it had to be done.

Breeders, she knew, had a powerful effect on demons, but Felicia was on an entirely different level. Norya hadn't just witnessed this, either; she'd *experienced* it. Though she wouldn't have minded a sexy romp with the cute little redhead in any other circumstance, being around Felicia had filled Norya with an unstoppable NEED to fuck her. Even missing the necessary parts to breed the girl, the raw, driving need to try had driven the she-demon to a point bordering madness. She hadn't been surprised that Shik had gotten to Felicia first—the horny orange imp was prone to fucking fruit and lost articles of clothing, so it was an inevitable fact that arrival of a flesh-and-blood pussy would have him running in with a cock that was harder than Hell-iron—and she supposed that, as the second-most horny member of the group, that meant it was no surprise to anyone that she'd gotten drawn in to Felicia's depths after Shik. But it said something that Zaiden had succumbed as quickly as he had. Granted, Norya had been expecting it—had been *hoping* for it, in fact—but, knowing how Zaiden felt about her, she'd been ready for disappointment. As it turned out, however, Zaiden hadn't just *not* been able to resist the breeder's pull, he hadn't even made it very far with her before convincing himself that they needed to go somewhere private.

"—to hide!" he'd defended when Norya had given him a knowing look during his explanation on their way back.

But she'd known better. Norya had watched Zaiden drag himself greater distances with worse injuries for the sake of less, so she wasn't about to go believing the lie that Zaiden was still convinced was the truth. It wasn't. No, the truth was that it had been the influences of the breeder tugging at his subconscious like the strings on a puppet. Such was the effect that breeders had, but there was something different about Felicia. Her breeder pull was stronger. It worked faster and spread further. And the effects it had: so immediate and so powerful that they'd compelled even a dedicated and disciplined soldier to believe he needed a place to rest.

Immediate and powerful enough to drag the long-dormant Alpha instincts out of their leader. She and

Varian had come face-to-face, started getting more and more heated in their hateful argument with one another —likely riling up all sorts of carnal instincts in him that he was struggling to understand—when suddenly that massive demon had come smashing through their wall, giving him a thorough jostling and, with it, a heavy dose of rage.

The perfect ingredients for what they'd wound up with: an out-of-control, *feral* Alpha.

And, though it was only a temporary solution at best, getting Varian to let out all that pent-up energy and rage and—judging from the size of the load in Norya's belly— "Alpha jelly" was the only way to calm him down and bring him back. With how he'd gotten, she'd known that things were bound to get ugly if she let him have a go at Felicia. Nevermind the savagery that had overcome him as a result of being around her, Norya couldn't begin to justify forcing Felicia to satisfy a demon she'd just gotten through telling she hated a short time earlier. That left the only option being what she would have otherwise been thrilled to perform...

But the only way to get Varian to go through with such a thing was to use everything she knew about him— everything he'd confided to her in his most vulnerable moments—to force him to submit and let her finish the job.

She'd felt dirty thinking it through, felt dirtier planning out the words and finally speaking them aloud, and she'd since felt utterly disgusting for how perfectly it had worked.

Because no sooner had Varian busted that pent-up

Alpha rage-nut straight down Norya's throat than he was back to his brooding-yet-brilliant self. As the Varian she'd known and loved for so long rose back up to occupy the deep, silver orbs of his eyes, she'd seen him fly through a flurried range of emotions. In the seconds that followed her final gulp, she'd seen rage and disgust, then nervousness and uncertainty, and finally shame. Dirty as she was feeling, she hadn't been able to offer him any of her typical assurances, all-too-certain he'd cut her off the moment she tried and accuse her of getting what they both knew she'd always wanted.

And she had always wanted it...

Just not like that.

So Norya had stayed quiet and let him arrive at his own conclusions, and it had made her feel even dirtier that, after all *that,* he'd actually understood; actually *agreed* with the decision and the method even though it had obviously hurt him terribly.

Because that's just the sort of leader he is, she'd thought with a horrible mixture of admiration and disgust.

Then, because it was what they both wanted—what they both *needed*—they wordlessly agreed to ignore the terrible awkwardness of what had just taken place between them. Norya recapped everything that had happened, telling Varian of how she'd overheard him and the breeder squabbling in the now-destroyed meeting room, how she'd seen the giant demon snatch up Felicia after burying him in debris, and then she explained everything that had happened after that. She opted to avoid the word "feral," but she made it clear enough how bad things had gotten that she was sure he was thinking it for himself by the end. She also made certain to use the word "boss" twice as much as usual, knowing that Varian already hated it when she called him that, but wanting to affirm that, regardless of what had just taken place—regardless of the awful, degrading words she'd used to make it happen—she didn't want the dynamic between them to change.

Norya still loved Varian, and she hoped that maybe this ugly moment might offer a sliver of opportunity for better things between them eventually, but she couldn't bear the thought of that dirty, desperate act changing what they already had.

Not when there was still work to be done, and definitely not when who-knew how many new troubles were coming their way.

She told him everything, and he listened to her. She watched his mind work with each new detail, and she paused to answer the occasional question or clarify the occasional confusion. As she began to detail the revelation she'd had about him being an Alpha, she'd watched Varian's eyes go wide, his brow furrow as though he was preparing to argue, and then his body slacken as he submitted to the obvious: Norya wouldn't be mistaken about something like that. She'd paused and waited as he had, momentarily compelled to ask for her own clarification when she heard him mutter, *"So* that's *why they pulled away when I yelled,"* to himself, but decided it was better to ignore it and went on to explain the confrontation in the basement and the blow that had knocked him out.

"... but, I mean, at least now your horns aren't uneven anymore, right, boss?" she'd wrapped up with a sheepish chuckle and a single, broad-shoulder shrug. "And, like you said, they will grow back."

Varian, likely only realizing in that moment that his lone horn had, in fact, been broken off, prodded at the jagged stumps on his head with the pads of his fingers before loosing a long, tired sigh.

Finally, looking more tired than she'd seen him in a long time, he asked, "Where's the breeder now?"

Norya frowned at that. "She *does* have a name, boss," she scolded, though she was secretly thankful to have the tone between them slipping back towards normal. "It's Feli—"

"Where?" Varian demanded, but his voice was—*thankfully*—still his own and not that horribly compelling Alpha command.

"Kaishu's treating her wounds," she answered with a sigh, "and you're going to *let* him treat her wounds." She fixed him with a look that she hoped wasn't too much like the one she'd just used to make him submit and fuck her face as she pushed further: "We both know that something's bound to happen between them—I can't imagine Kaishu's will is going to prevent him from succumbing to what Zaiden and even you couldn't—but you're just going to have to let—"

Varian's lip curled as he looked away. Norya could tell that he didn't like the idea, but she could also tell that his head was clear enough that he couldn't come up with any rational reason not to like the idea. Submitting to this, he justified the interruption with, "I don't care what either of them do. Doesn't mean I have to like it."

"I wouldn't expect you to, boss," Norya offered, starting to reach a hand towards his knee before catching the cold look he gave her at the sight. Biting her lip, she whimpered and retracted her arm.

A sticky, weird silence clung between them.

Varian tugged at the leg of his pants as though they were fitting funny since he'd rushed to put them on.

Norya cleared her throat and tried to hide the intoxicating reminder that some of his cum was still clinging there.

Finally, hating the silence for how loudly it advertised what was making her feel so dirty, she finally asked, "You're okay then? You don't need anything else from me?"

Clearly relieved for the shift—as well as an obvious exit from the awkwardness—Varian gave her his most convincing *"I'm the boss"*-face and nodded. "I am, yes. You're fine to go." Then, in a wavering display that had him looking a lot like he had back when Norya found him in that ditch, he called back, "And... err, Norya?"

Fighting to suppress a shiver at his tone, Norya forced herself to meet his suddenly shimmering gaze. "Yeah, boss?"

It was his turn to clear his throat. "I, uh... well, I'm glad you're with me—with *us,* I mean. It..." he paused and worked his jaw before looking down at his laced fingers. "It sounds like you served as a great leader in my absence, and I... err—I-I appreciate you making the hard decisions that you did. I know you probably hated having to make them, but..." he looked back up at her and nodded, giving her an old, friendly smile as he did. "They were the right decisions, and I really appreciate everything you did for us tonight." Then, in an uncharacteristically shy whisper, he added, "A-and everything you d-did... f-for me."

Norya's mouth went dry on a soundless gasp, and her lungs began to instantly burn as she held the breath for a moment, sampling the words and feeling her insides flutter as she did. Finally, letting the air out nice-and-slow, she returned the smile and the nod. "You know you never have to thank me for any of that, Varian," she said, then immediately felt her cheeks go solar as the deeper meaning behind those words reverberated between them. Eager to get out, not wanting him to see whatever emotion she was starting to feel tearing at the forefronts of her mind, she stood and started for his door. "Now get some rest," she ordered before adding as an afterthought, "boss."

Varian didn't reply, but they both knew that there was no reply that would serve the purpose. She knew he wouldn't risk confronting Kaishu and putting himself that close to the breeder again, and he knew that she couldn't bear to be that close to him any longer.

They were both thankful that she was leaving.
He obviously hated the turn things had taken.
And Norya...
Norya hated how cold he kept his room.

CHAPTER 12
FEELING KNOTTY

Felicia wasn't sure how long she'd been out, but she was pleasantly surprised by two facts as she came out of it:

For one, she wasn't having any nightmares or suffering any of those mind-tearing headaches.

And, for another, she actually felt somewhat rested.

This second fact arrived as consciousness had her recalling how she'd been feeling just before everything had gone dark. She'd been drop-dead tired, ping-ponging between uncontrollable horniness and unbearable pain, and she'd been feeling sympathetic for Zaiden. Between the perils of his past and the emotions he was obviously struggling with towards Norya, Felicia had almost surprised herself at how easy it had been to connect with the demon. Though she hadn't registered it at the time, she remembered distantly wondering if she'd been an empathetic person before she'd arrived in Hell. She hated not knowing who she was—who she'd *been*—in her prior life, but she had to believe that she must have been a good person if her first instinct while listening to Zaiden was to feel sorry for him.

The since unthought conditional of *"But good people don't wind up in Hell"* threatened to dawn on the horizon of her mind, but that had been when Varian had arrived and...

And had me cumming so hard that it felt like my body was going to tear itself apart! she thought.

And it was this thought that served as her first wholly complete one as she started to come to, realizing first that the pain she'd been in before was gone and that she wasn't waking up to any of the normal horrors she'd been plagued by since her arrival. It was pleasant, as was the aroma that fanned across her nostrils as her senses followed her into waking. It was like the rain at night, and even this thought came and went without even a splinter of a headache. Her eyelids fluttered with a momentary uncertainty, remembering how painful shards of light had been for her the past few times she'd opened her eyes in Hell. Instead of bright, burning agony, however, she was met with a soothing dimness that felt as pleasant to her vision as a cool breeze on a warm day. She heard herself hum contentedly at that and bit down on her breath, holding it and waiting to see what fresh chaos the sound might have invited. Nothing happened. Another wave of relief passed, and she let out the breath, feeling as though a great weight was slipping away with it.

"Are you still asleep?" a voice that she could only think of as "shadowy" called to her.

An old joke bubbled to the surface of her thoughts, nothing now but a cluster of words with no certain origin, and she thought, *The only question you can't answer "yes" to.* They were silly words with an even sillier meaning. Felicia was certain there were other questions like that, the most immediate one being, *Are you dead?*

This thought didn't give Felicia a headache, but it did flood her with a confusing wave of giddiness and dread. Her eyes snapped open, certain that she was about to either begin laughing or screaming uncontrollably, but all that came out was another relaxing breath and, with it, an answer to the shadow's question:

"No. I... I don't think so."

And, ridiculous as that answer sounded even to her, she couldn't argue with her own doubt. Since arriving in Hell, every moment of waking or thinking had been met with pain. Finding herself pain-free in that instant seemed like reason enough to doubt, but too much else felt real—felt *awake*—to let her indulge in the belief that she was dreaming.

Besides, pain or no, Felicia still felt horny...

But at least it was a calm horny this time.

The shadow gave a soft pitter of laughter, and then it extended a limb made of darkness and set something warm and damp on Felicia's forehead. She gave a soft-yet-startled yelp at the sight of living darkness before her eyes refocused and saw a clear divide between the shadow and the body occupying it.

Kaishu!

It seemed strange to Felicia to realize that she'd come to remember his name long before having a face to put it to. Prior to that moment, everything to do with Kaishu had been a dark blur with that title or the title occupying a space that its owner had already vanished from. Considering this, she realized that it was no wonder she'd been thinking of him as a sort of living darkness, but now, standing before her and *not* already gone or in the midst of vanishing yet again, she saw that there was much more than just empty darkness to this demon.

He was long and slender and dark. Once more, Felicia's thoughts grabbed at a pair of words—*"fox"* and *"ninja"*—and, though she couldn't quite recall their meaning, she felt somehow confident that they described the demon before her perfectly. She also felt an overwhelming relief that those words had come and gone from her mind without a single twinge of a headache.

Still can't remember a damned thing, she thought, reaching up to touch whatever Kaishu had just placed on her brow, *but at least it doesn't feel like torture to try to remember.*

Her fingers sank into something spongy, and, as they did, she felt a small pool of warmth grow beneath each fingertip. After another moment of experimental prodding, she decided that it was a damp cloth. As her hand retreated, though, she realized that there was more to it: several brownish droplets clinging to the pads of her pointer and middle fingers telling her it was more than just simple water. She rubbed her thumb against first one and then the other, then gave the trio a tentative sniff, finding the aroma strangely familiar.

"Tea," Kaishu offered, his four eyes regarding her curiosity with a hesitant curiosity of their own.

Felicia caught herself staring back at them, captivated by the light-blue orbs and how, despite being so utterly alien on that already strangely beautiful animal-like face, she felt even more comforted by them. Adding to this demon's surreal appearance and its equally surreal calming effect was his horns:

All the other demons in Varian's crew had horns that flared upward or outward. Even the bright and bouncy Shik's small, single horn rose up from his forehead. Kaishu's horns, however, hung out just over his brow, punctuating the topmost pair of eyes, and then curved downward in a hooding effect. These horns, almost seeming to bow, framed either side of his pointed face and lent to his already long and lanky appearance.

Again, Felicia thought *"fox"* and *"ninja,"* and, again, these thoughts were met without any of the normal pain. Then she thought, *Beautiful!* before once more looking at her fingertips and repeating, "Tea?"

The bowing horns on the bluish-purple fox-ninja dipped with the rest of his face as he nodded. "It's not easy to get, especially not here, but I have my sources," he explained. Then, nodding back towards her forehead, he said, "When it's boiled down and concentrated, it helps with stress and headaches." He shrugged then and gave an awkward grin. "It's good for sore muscles, too, so I like to soak my feet in it after missions."

Felicia felt her lips curl in a curious grin, and she once more reached for the tea-dampened cloth. "This isn't the same tea you...?" she began, leading the question rather than finishing it.

The sides of Kaishu's face brightened to a shade of plum and then back again as he shook his head. "N-no. No! I swear, I wouldn't—" he stopped himself and gave another of those soft, pittering laughs. "Sorry, no. I..." his face went plum again as his four eyes danced first away from her, then at her chest, then away again before finally arriving back on her face. "Apologies. I am not great at jokes."

Felicia's grin evolved into a gentle smile, and she shrugged. "Seems only fair," she offered, "since you seem to be great at a lot of other stuff." She hooded her eyes and took in another deep, relaxing breath. "Including making Hell feel *not* like Hell."

Another round of pitters followed with another strangely beautiful smile. "You're very nice to say so. Very nice," he said in that shadowy voice. His eyes darted again—moving with all the speed and grace as the rest of him—and Felicia nearly missed him stealing another glance at her chest before looking back into her eyes. "V-very nice."

Felicia, both eerily flattered by his shy, darting glances as well as now practically bathing in that calm horniness, did nothing to discourage them. She felt her own cheeks warm up a little as she moved to sit up a little more and took a moment to study her surroundings. She spotted a short table with a wide, shallow bowl that appeared to contain the concentrated tea for her forehead. Next to this, she caught sight of a wisp of smoke curling away from the glowing tip of a stick of incense. Opposite this was a small, modest cot with what looked like a nest of tangled quilts and blankets. The room itself was mostly empty besides those few bits of furniture, but, before she could fully complete that thought—before she'd ultimately decided that the room was, in fact, empty

—she started to notice all the banners and tapestries hanging on the walls. Some were plain and simple with symbols that she couldn't read scrawled across them, but a few clashed so much against these that it had her remembering all over again how different Kaishu was from the already eclectic group. These few-yet-radically-different pieces of wall-art appeared to be posters, and, upon closer inspection, Felicia found her mind grabbing at another word that she didn't understand but still felt strangely right:

"Circus."

Those four eyes followed the line of Felicia's sight, caught her staring at an illustration that seemed to show a demon like Kaishu leaping over a series of burning obstacles set above an impossibly thin wire. Seeing it cemented the certainty that the room was Kaishu's—that it wasn't just another random basement or other such happenstance keep that she'd found herself in with a member of the demon crew—and she realized that they must have taken back to the building that the giant demon had snatched her from.

"My family," he said in that low, shadowy voice.

"Huh?" Felicia squawked, embarrassing herself and looking back at him.

Kaishu, still looking at the poster, nodded towards it and repeated, "My family." Then, steering his fox-like head back in her direction, he clarified: "Performers. All of us. We were acrobats and... erm, *teloch ber*—no..." he furrowed his brow—something that reminded Felicia of a timid animal—and then shrugged and tittered again. "I believe the best word you would understand is—*heh*—

'daredevil.' You know, one who risks harm and even death to entertain others, yes?"

"I..." Felicia began, blushed at her own thoughts, and finally blanched at confessing what she'd been worrying over all along: "I can't remember anything from... well, from before. Before I was here, I mean. Even trying to remember words from there..." she trailed off as a new weight of despair began to settle over her.

Kaishu cocked his head and considered before reaching out and setting a palm against the cloth. The additional pressure sent a bead of moisture running down Felicia's temple, but the calming sensation was too intoxicating to spoil by worrying over something as insubstantial and momentary as a single droplet. She heard a gentle hum, realized it was her letting out another contented sigh, and did nothing to suppress this, either.

"Headache," he said.

Though it didn't sound like a question, Felicia still hummed, "Mmhm," and then opened her eyes to study him. "W-wait..." she pondered aloud. "How did you know that? I haven't..." she stopped there, not sure what it was she might've said or done to give it away—least of all to Kaishu—but still certain that she couldn't have given him any clues to her ailment.

He shrugged, worked the cloth over each of her temples, and finally withdrew it and set it back in the shallow bowl to soak. "Pain is easy to spot in people," he said. "Even easier for denizens of Hell. We are..." he lingered to sneer at his own words before finishing, "... *better* at the tasks of torture for it." He glanced back at her as if awaiting judgement.

Felicia didn't give him any. If anything, she found herself feeling sad for him. All the same, however...

"Why do demons torture people?" she blurted.

Kaishu, almost seeming to expect the question, shrugged and said, "For the same reason the angels comfort them, and for the same reason that those in your realm spend their brief lives struggling with the choices that will send them here or there. To others, our purposes might seem simple or even mundane, but they still find a way to fit together with the roles that beings from each realm occupy." He gave a quick smirk, and Felicia caught his eyes doing another sweep to her chest and back again before he looked back at the—*circus*—poster. "Like my family and all others who dedicate their lives to entertaining others, it can seem silly or even stupid if you don't see how what they're doing correlates to others. My family played with death so that others could feel excitement with risk. Your people play with sins so that angels and demons can feel relevant by rewarding or punishing them for it. And maybe there's another layer beyond it— maybe many more still—acting upon the outcomes of what we do here the way we act upon the outcome of what you do."

Felicia blinked at that and gave a nervous giggle. "Did you just explain the meaning of *everything* by comparing it to a... a..." she looked back at the poster and thought again, *"circus."*

Kaishu shrugged again. "Perhaps. Or perhaps I am wrong. It makes sense to me to think of it that way, because it was the life I knew. If my family had baked pies for the nobles and elites, then perhaps I would say that existence is like feeding people, but my family were not bakers, and so I don't see existence that way. In either case, existence is not difficult to understand. Difficult to survive, yes, and even more difficult to find joy within, but not to understand. You know this, yes?" he nodded those bowing horns to her again, and, again, his eyes took a sip from her chest before rising again. "Just as I see the pain of confusion—the pain of the headaches—in you, I see that you are painfully aware, as well. Perhaps not of where you came from or where you are, but you feel the hurt of knowing that this is real. And, truly, there's little else in any existence that anybody can know. Like entertainment, the rest of what we call life is just a performance: just costumes and illusions." He looked back at the poster and chewed his lip for a moment before whispering in that shadowy voice, "We can only hope that the seats we find to watch the show are ones beside people we might come to love and admire."

Felica balked at that. "You're... not at all what I would have expected you to be," she finally confessed.

Kaishu nodded and hummed again. "You thought I would be like an angry animal, yes? Many of your kind think that of my kin when they first arrive. They will sometimes say, 'wolf' or 'fox' or sometimes 'dog'—a most peculiar confusion, as Varian's kind are usually the ones referred to as such, but Varian, for whatever reason, does not look like the rest of his kind—but the most accurate description your world has for my kin is 'whisperer.'" He made a sound like a purr and scooched closer as he lived up to this title by lowering his voice to say, "Back in a time when your kind needed more convincing to play with sin, it was my kind that would cross over in the night to plant thoughts. We had to fast and stealthy then—had to be part of the darkness; had to be voices that made no sound—and we had to know how to *not* be where we were a moment before. We became very good at this—very, very good, yes?—but, as your people came to need less and less motivation, my kind were needed less and less. Finally, we found ourselves without that greater purpose, and all that was left was..." his eyes finished by trailing back to the poster.

"I'm sorry," Felicia whispered back.

"I am not," Kaishu said, still staring at the poster. "I always thought entertainment to be better than corruption. Unfortunately, in this place, the only ones who get to be entertained are the elites and nobles, the cruelest of the cruel. In my opinion, they are the ones who need entertainment the least, and it is also my opinion that they are the least deserving of it. Especially since—" he stopped himself, blinked first one set of eyes and then the other, and finally looked away from the poster.

His gaze landed once again on Felicia's chest, but it lingered there longer than before.

For some reason, this struck Felicia as sad, as well, and she reached out to put her hand on his. "Since what?" she prompted him.

He blinked again, and when his lids lifted his eyes were once more on hers. "Since it was the ones my family was entertaining who took their lives for their own entertainment." There was a low, almost inaudible rumble in his throat that Felicia didn't register as a growl until it was over. Then, shrugging again, he said, "It is why I am not an entertainer; why I've put those skills that were once good for whispering to being an assassin and working with Varian to be a plague on the elites and nobles. And, with good fortune, perhaps we will become legends of Hell like Lucifer's fall or the wars of the realms or the eternal hunt for Princess Isadora and the other Twelve Heretics. It will no doubt be long after we are gone, but—"

"STOP!" Felicia yelled, grabbing Kaishu by the wrists with a startling speed and strength. Between the volume and the force, the outburst had the whispering demon barking in surprise. She wanted to apologize—almost felt ridiculous for the outburst—but...

"The Princess"? Was that... yes. YES! That's what it said, she thought, nodding to herself, *and it said her name was—*

"'Isadora,'" she repeated. "That... that *thing* that took me, it told me I *smelled* like the princess; like Isadora! It said that it guarded her—that she was 'one of the twelve'—and that, of those twelve, she was one-of-six that it guarded. What does that mean? Who is Princess Isadora? Who are the Twelve Heretics?"

Kaishu stared, stunned, and went on awkwardly blinking those four eyes in bewilderment. "I..." he began, then shrugged and shook his head. "I do not know. Apologies. I only know that there are stories—long-old stories, mind you; what your world might call 'fairytales'—of Twelve Heretics and, of them, of a princess named Isadora being among the first. I don't recall much of the stories, but it was said that she was wild and rebellious. I believe there was something of her 'still shining from her father's blessing,' but that is a poor translation that many interpret in different ways. Some believe it means her father—a king, one would imagine—gave some sort of gift to his daughter, while others believe it meant that she somehow benefited from a gift that had been given to him, and still others insist that it means an angel must have blessed their family, starting with the father. Then again," Kaishu offered another shrug and an apologetic look as he said, "many think it just means that the king and the princess were prone to acts of incest, and that these encounters often left her 'glowing,' as is a phrase I hear your people are fond of using."

Felicia, feeling suddenly like a balloon that was starting to run out of air, began to—

The pain was back, ripping and searing through her head. It demanded to know what a *"balloon"* was; how she knew of such a thing, how such a thing could have air, let alone "run out" of it. She rocked against the pain, whimpered, and found herself clinging to Kaishu as it started to fade again.

"Y-you... you're in pain, yes?" asked the fox-nin—
GAH!—
The demon!

Felicia groaned and nodded, her chest aching and burning; heaving. She felt Kaishu's eyes darting again, and this time she caught his sight on the return trip and grinned through the ache. "My existence here *is* pain, Kaishu," she said, recalling the strange peace he'd made her feel in tending to her and speaking to her.

That calm horniness was still calm, but it was refusing to be ignored now.

Kaishu had been kind and patient. He'd rid her of the pain of her existence in Hell for a longer stretch of time than any other, and for that...

"Will you undress for me, Kaishu?" she asked him in a low, shadowy whisper. "I'd like to thank you for what you've done for me... yes?"

Those four eyes widened and a new sort of titter emerged. Kaishu stammered for a moment, then he struggled to look away. He got as far as Felicia's tits again. "I... I do not," he whimpered even as his head began to nod slowly. "Y-you do not need to—"

"I *want* to thank you, Kaishu," Felicia purred, pulling his hands back within her grasp and planting them on her chest, letting him cup what he'd been stealing glances at since she'd woken up. Then, gasping at the almost electric rush of the contact, she revised: "I *need* to fuck you!"

Then, because she knew that he wasn't going to do it himself, she moved to pull off the shirt she'd found herself in. Being unconscious for the trip back, she wasn't sure whose it was or when it had been placed on her, but the questions surrounding it were forgotten as quickly as it took to remove it and cast it aside. Kaishu's gaze flashed with excitement at the sight, and his hands began to work her tits before he even seemed to register the movement.

Felicia moaned, leaned into the contact—feeling the lingering pain of the headache vanish as she did—and then she began to pull off the fox-ninja's clothes. They were, though she had no way of knowing how she knew this, appropriate for the title: tight-fitting and black. Though it was hard to tell before where his outfit ended and his dark-skinned body began, she quickly discovered his flesh to be far more beautiful without the confining layers. His lean, long torso emerged and, suddenly needing to taste it, she leaned in and ran her teeth over one of his nipples.

Kaishu gave a nervous, almost ticklish gasp at that and flexed against the contact, clearly uncertain how to react.

The shy, withdrawn gestures only spurred Felicia further. She drew back, spotted another set of nipples below the first, and yet another below that, and she cooed at the realization that his bestial features weren't reserved just to his fox-like head. Made all the curious by this discovery—suddenly very eager to see Kaishu's cock and even more eager to feel it—she kissed, licked, and nipped her way down, pausing to pay tribute to each of his nipples along the way while her hands made short work of his pants. By the time her face had reached his lap, she had just released him in all of his glory.

The treatment had him half-erect already, and she was titillated to find herself slightly disappointed at not seeing what it looked like at rest. At that moment, however, she was greeted by a cock that was long, pinkish, and already shining with moisture. At its base, she spotted what looked like a pocket of flesh, and, staring on in horny fascination, she saw more and more of that cock emerging, growing thicker and darker and shinier as it did. The rigidity alarmed her, and she wondered if it ever truly softened or if it just shrank down enough to vanish into that pocket.

Before she could think too deeply on the glorious anatomy of Kaishu, however, she caught a hot, warm shot of liquid across her cheek and yelped in surprise and glee. "Oh my! Are you already cummi—" she began before another shot caught her in the mouth, silencing her with a wave of salty sweetness. She groaned, felt herself orgasm a bit at just the taste, and then closed her lips around the tip and waited for another spurt.

She didn't have to wait long.

Kaishu whimpered, loosed another pleasured bark, and another squirt of the stuff shot across the length of Felicia's tongue.

"Ooh! So good! You feed me so good, baby," she moaned, pulling back and marveling at how much thicker and darker his cock had grown in that brief interlude.

It was now bright red and almost as thick as her wrist. Moreover, another few inches had emerged, and, with them—

"HOLY FUCK!" she moaned at the new sight, already starting to cum on herself despite not knowing what she was looking at.

There, at the base of Kaishu's already sizable, still-spurting cock, was a large, round bulb that appeared to be pulsing like a heartbeat.

A nervous, shy whimper slipped past the demon as he whispered, "M-my knot..."

"A knot?" Felicia repeated, studying it for a moment before finally moving to run her fingertips over it. No sooner had she made contact with the flared base than Kaishu moaned—his loudest one yet—and a fresh shot of that sweet, hot liquid caught her across the nose and splashed across the rest of her face.

"I... I am sorry," he called down, trembling out of embarrassment and pleasure. "I did not mean—*AHH!*"

Felicia wasn't about to entertain his apologies. The mini-facial had made given her another mini-orgasm, and she returned the favor by lunging forward and dragging her tongue across the topside of the demon's knot, cooing and giggling as he moaned again and shot another batch over her shoulder and halfway to the wall behind her.

"Ooh, Kaishu," she panted up at him. "That is *sooo* fucking sexy!" She gave it another lick, marveled as it earned another squirt, and then asked, "I-is it... is it just for pleasure then? Should I—*mm!*—focus my attention on it?"

"O-ooh! W-wait," he begged, clearly overwhelmed by the sensation.

Pouting, Felicia did.

"Mmm," Kaishu groaned as two more heavy shots squirted out without any provocation, then, working to settle himself, he nodded and said, "M-my knot is sensitive, yes, b-but... *mmph!*" he groaned again, and another squirt rocketed out.

Already expecting it this time, Felicia moved her face to take it across her lips and moaned at the wave of flavor.

"Oh my..." Kaishu groaned at the display before working to continue: "My knot feels good, b-but it's meant to..." that plum glow returned to his face as he stammered a bit more. "I-it's meant to 'tie' me to a female during mating. It enters her, and it swells up and... you see—"

Realization dawned on Felica as the ability to speak seemed to leave the demon. Her eyes went wide. Her pussy clenched hungrily. "So this beautiful thing goes inside me, gets even bigger and fatter, and then stretches me... from the *inside?*"

"N-not just stretching," Kaishu corrected, but he was nodding all the same. "It *ties* us," he said, and the explanation motivated another blast.

This one missed Felicia's mouth, skirting her cheek and vanishing into her hair. She groaned at the loss, but felt a spike of dirty glee at knowing she was getting showered in her lupine lover's juices. "Mm! 'Tied,' huh?" she repeated, already starting to lie on her back and spread her legs.

A brief glance confirmed that her pussy had flooded and drenched her thighs halfway to her knees.

The view had Kaishu squirting another three rounds: one catching a bullseye on her left nipple, the second cascading across her belly, and the last splashing into her pubic hair.

She thought, *Getting closer to your target, baby!* and instinctively spread her cunt lips with her fingers.

Kaishu, still nodding, started to move towards her as though in a trance. Not seeming to notice that he was already closing in, he continued with his explanation: "When I'm tied to you... I won't be able to pull out, a-and you'll be stuck to me until I'm spent."

Felicia moaned at the idea of it and nodded, bucking her hips up to meet his spurting cock. "You don't have to sell me on it anymore, baby! Just hurry the fuck up and stuff it in me!"

A louder, more hungry growl emerged from the fox-ninja's throat as he lowered himself over her, his cockhead vanishing between her folds. The moment he was inside her, another round of squirting started. Felicia felt them collide against the walls of her pussy, the sensation sending her over the edge again. As more and more of Kaishu's cock entered—sending more and more squirts deeper and deeper into her—she became evermore aware of each orgasmic constriction until...

"O-oh! OH! OH, FUCK, KAISHU! FUCK! YOU'RE—*AAAAHH!*" she howled as she felt the fat, fist-sized knot slip in and swell even more. It felt as though he'd taken up every available inch of space in her clenching cunt, and then gone on to get even bigger. She lost track of her orgasms, lost track of where one ended and another began.

Then, feeling a wave of ironic bliss at the realization that he'd helped awaken her a moment earlier, she realized that the orgasmic assault was actually making her pass out again...

I suppose existence in Hell could be worse than this, she thought, feeling yet another massive squirt from her demon-lover flooding her pussy and inflating her insides like a balloon. **A lot** *worse!*

CHAPTER 13
DETECTIVE DEXTER...
IN HELL!

Dexter groaned and struggled to get a handle on what was happening. He'd been falling, yes—falling down the stairs of his house in an effort to get away from that bitch, Karen—but he distinctly remembered that fall ending. It had ended, and he'd been looking back up the stairs at—

But then why was I falling again?

And again?

And...

Now, just coming out of another round of falling, Dexter was *still* looking up at...

There were no stairs, and there was definitely no Karen.

He was at the bottom of some sort of pit, lying in a giant, dusty ring surrounded by towering rock walls. And there, standing over him the same way Karen had been standing over him at the top of the stairs, was a...

Woman?

She had all the parts, Dexter supposed, but there was

still something about her that seemed to defy the title. The immediate detail that he noticed before everything else was her tits. They were pointy. *Too* pointy. They looked sharp, almost lethal, beneath a thin, unnatural-looking dress.

And then there's her skin, he thought, squinting to try to figure it out. *It's... pink?*

And yes, it was. It wasn't an unnatural, artificial-looking tone, either—not like the body paint that was so popular with cosplayers at conventions—but, instead, looked more like the tasty, succulent pink of a woman who had her best parts spread open on a porno site.

She's the color of a pussy! Dexter marveled. *And her hair looks like strands of silver!*

Still not sure who—*or what*—this woman was, Dexter had already decided that he would move Heaven and...

Dexter gulped, flooded by a sudden and terrible sense of knowing, one that did nothing to quell his instant love for this—*DEMON!*—woman.

"Wh-who..." he croaked from a throat that felt dried from a thousand years without use. "Who are you?"

"Me?" the—*DEMON!*—woman chirped down at him with a laugh. "Darling, you *must* be new here to not know that already," she taunted, squatting down and peering over the ledge for a closer look.

Dexter gasped as he realized that she wasn't wearing any panties beneath that dress; that he could clearly see her pussy between her casually splayed knees as she considered him further.

Yes. Yes, he was certain now that he was in love with her.

Again, he croaked out, "Who...?"

Though she clearly noticed him staring, she did nothing to hide herself from his view as she called down, "I am Saroya, and if you've fallen here—straight into my own arena—then that means I am your new queen."

Dexter didn't need to be a detective to arrive at the conclusion that this must be Heaven.

ALSO AVAILABLE BY NATHAN SQUIERS:

CRIMSON SHADOW SERIES:

Noir

Sins of the Father

Forbidden Dance

Dance with the Devil

The Longest Night

Gods & Monsters

New World Order

OTHER WORKS:

Scarlet Night

(co-authored with Megan J. Parker)

Scarlet Dawn

(co-authored with Megan J. Parker)

Scarlet Dusk

(co-authored with Megan J. Parker)

A Howl at the Moon

Death, Death, and the Dying Day: A Weird West Story

Twisted Words & Melted Thoughts: A Poetry & Song Collection

The Winter Sun

(co-authored with Megan J. Parker)

New Moon: A Paranormal Reverse Harem Novel

(co-authored with Megan J. Parker)

Original Sin & Scarlet Rising: A Crimson Shadow & Behind the Vail Story

(co-authored with Megan J. Parker)

Running on Empty: The Crows MC #1

(co-authored with Megan J. Parker)

Riding on Fumes: The Crows MC #2

(co-authored with Megan J. Parker)

Braking Down: The Crows MC #3

(co-authored with Megan J. Parker)

Journey to YOUR Story: A start-to-finish guide for your personal writing journey

(co-authored with Megan J. Parker)

Black Man White Man

(co-authored with Joe Janowicz)

About Nathan Squiers

Nathan Squiers is a resident of Upstate New York, where he divides his time not-so-equally at home between writing and "nerding out" over comic books, anime, and horror movie marathons with his loving wife and fellow author, Megan J. Parker, and their "fur babies." When he isn't lost in the realm of fiction, Nathan can usually be found at the gym, furthering his efforts as an amateur powerlifter.

A four-time USA Today bestselling and award-winning author, Nathan Squiers began his writing career in 2012 and was voted one of the top-ten new authors of that year. His debut novel, Curtain Call, received both the "Best Occult" and "Best Paranormal Thriller" awards with the Blogger Book Fair, and his Crimson Shadow series has gone on to gain international recognition and become a bestseller in urban fantasy and dark fantasy.

Visit Nathan Squiers' website to learn more about him and his works.

Made in the USA
Middletown, DE
04 November 2024